William Dean Howells

Sketch of the Life and Character of Rutherford B. Hayes

William Dean Howells

Sketch of the Life and Character of Rutherford B. Hayes

ISBN/EAN: 9783743348936

Manufactured in Europe, USA, Canada, Australia, Japa

Cover: Foto ©Raphael Reischuk / pixelio.de

Manufactured and distributed by brebook publishing software (www.brebook.com)

William Dean Howells

Sketch of the Life and Character of Rutherford B. Hayes

SKETCH

OF THE

LIFE AND CHARACTER

OF

RUTHERFORD B. HAYES.

By WM. D. HOWELLS.

ALSO A BIOGRAPHICAL SKETCH OF

WILLIAM A. WHEELER.

WITH PORTRAITS OF BOTH CANDIDATES

NEW YORK:
PUBLISHED BY HURD AND HOUGHTON.
BOSTON: H. O. HOUGHTON AND COMPANY.
Cambridge: The Riverside Press.
1876.

PREFACE.

THIS book is my own enterprise, and has been in nowise adopted or patronized by the man whose life and character I have tried to portray.

It differs chiefly from the biographies already before the public, in the large use made of original letters, diaries, note-books and scrap-books placed at my disposal without restriction and without instruction. In this use I have been guided solely by my own sense of fitness and my respect for the just limits of personality, on which I hope not to have trenched, though I might have printed every word of his, and only the more commended Rutherford B. Hayes to the honor and affection of the people.

Written within four weeks after the material came to my hand, the book has, I know, very many faults of haste; but it was not in the power of any writer, however hurried or feeble, wholly to obscure the interest of that material; and whatever is the result of the political contest, I cannot think that people will quickly forget the story of a life so true and high.

I wish distinctly to say that General Hayes is responsible for no comment or construction of mine upon any word or act of his; and whatever is ambitious, or artificial, or unwise in my book is doubly my misfortune, for it is altogether false to him.

W. D. HOWELLS.

CAMBRIDGE, *September* 7, 1876.

CONTENTS.

CHAPTER IX.

CHAPTER X.

CHAPTER XI

CHAPTER XII.

LIFE AND CHARACTER

OF

RUTHERFORD B. HAYES.

CHAPTER I.

ANCESTRY AND CHILDHOOD.

"THE name of Hayes began by valor," wrote Mr. Ezekiel Hayes, of New Haven, scythe-maker, sometime in the last century ; and he goes on to tell how once, in a fight with the Danes, the retreating Scots came upon a husbandman and his two sons at work in the fields. " Pull your plow and harrow to pieces and fight ! " said the father, and with this timely succor — more remarkable for quality than quantity — the Danes were beaten ; and lands were bestowed upon the father for his bravery. "This man (my father's grandfather, George Hayes)," continues the too zealous genealogist, " went from Scotland to Derbyshire, in England, and lived with his uncle. He was anxious to see London, whither he went. Having received some account of America, he took passage and came to this country."

It was in 1682 that George Hayes settled in Wind-

sor, Connecticut, at which time, according to the ir-
reverent computations of a modern descendant of Mr.
Ezekiel Hayes, the veteran must have been some seven
hundred years old, since the battle in question took place
about 980. But the brave tradition is well found at
least; it was heartily accepted as part of the family
annals by the early Puritan Hayeses of Connecticut, and
its veracity ought not to be impeached because of their
confusion of mind respecting dates. It is, however, of
small importance to us who hope to elect General
Hayes President of the United States, how his name
began in Scotland so long ago. It continues in valor,
no matter how it began, and a man of his good New
England ancestry has nothing to crave of the Herald's
College. We hold rather by the Connecticut Hayeses
than by those of Scotland, and we need but briefly concern ourselves with any of the forefathers of a man
who is himself ancestor in the Napoleonic sense.

Little is known of George Hayes, who emigrated in
1682, beyond the fact that he settled first at Wind-
sor and afterwards removed to that part of Simsbury
which is now Granby. His son Daniel was taken by
the Indians about the year 1712, and carried captive to
Canada, whence he was ransomed by act of the Colonial Assembly appropriating " seven pounds to be paid
out of the public treasury " for that purpose. What
claim, if any, he had upon the colony's consideration,
by reason of civic prominence or military service, is not
asserted even by so ardent a genealogist as his son
Ezekiel, whom we have already quoted; probably he

was a plain, brave farmer, fighting in defense of his home, and was ransomed according to a general custom of the time, upon his "praying for some relief." It is known that he came home to Simsbury, and died there in 1756; but his son Ezekiel removed to New Haven, where the first Rutherford [1] Hayes, grandfather of our candidate, was born. This Rutherford was in due time apprenticed to a blacksmith, and, removing from New Haven first to New Hampshire and then to West Brattleborough, Vermont, he wrought at his trade there many years in a forge which the people built to welcome him, and became a man of substance, a farmer and innkeeper, dying in 1836, the father of eleven children. The fifth of these, Rutherford, was an active and enterprising spirit, and he was already a thrifty farmer and merchant when, in 1817, the West, which was even then beginning to be the Great West, tempted his energies. He emigrated to Delaware, Ohio, bought land, established himself in prosperous business, and five years later died of a typhoid fever, leaving a wife and two children. Some three months after, on the 4th of October, 1822, a son was born to him, and the widow called the child's name RUTHERFORD BIRCHARD HAYES, in memory of the father whose loss was yet so terribly new, and in grateful affection for that most loving brother [2] who was

[1] The surname of an ancestor on the female side, who came to New Haven in 1643, and from whose daughter's marriage proceed the New Haven Trowbridges.

[2] Sardis Birchard, who died a few years since, at Fremont, Ohio. He had lived unmarried, and in the course of a long life had amassed

thereafter a tender and devoted guardian of her father-less children.

It is of this Rutherford Birchard Hayes that the present sketch treats, with an inadequacy which the reader may feel, though he cannot know the keen re-gret of the writer, whom the rich material in the family records, the letters, and the diaries placed at his service tempts to a work far beyond the scope and limits of this.

The Hayeses of the colonial times, from whom we have here traced Rutherford B. Hayes's descent in the direct line, were a strong, brave, simple race, following the plow, wielding the hammer, and hewing out their way as plain men must in a new land. After the first emigrant, George Hayes, of Scotland, who may have been of a less rigid faith, they seem to have taken the prevailing tint of Connecticut Puritanism — always less blue than it has been painted; and thereafter, till Rutherford's time, the evangelists, and the judges, the prophets, and the kings of Israel supply the serious names of their Daniels, Ezekiels, Aarons, Joels, Mar-thas, Zilpahs, and Rebeccas; there was, indeed, one Silence Hayes of the third generation, but the conces-sion to imagination in her name is not in the liveliest spirit, and, considering that she was a woman, might

a large property, which General Hayes inherits. He was a man not only of good heart and of great practical force of character, but of the best public spirit and of cultivated tastes. He gave a library and a park to the town of Fremont, and left to his nephew a gallery of pict-ures including works by some of the best American and modern French and German painters.

appear a stroke of that grim irony which the auster-
est faith permits itself. So far as we can learn, the
Hayeses were never in public station and never enjoyed uncommon social distinction. /But they had
qualities of a sort apt, in an honest and thrifty stock,
when the moment comes, to flower into greatness / and
they had the gift, not yet extinct in their line, of winning superior women for their wives, through whom
they united themselves with families of worth, learning, and piety. Ezekiel married a Russell, of those
Russells who, first sojourning in Cambridge after their
emigration from England, followed the Reverend Mr.
Hooker into the Connecticut wilderness, when its first
church troubles distracted our good town. They remained men of character and of a consideration which
their Connecticut descendants still enjoy; but none has
so distinct a claim upon our honor as that son of the
original emigrant who concealed the fugitive Regicides
at Hadley many years, and of whom it is written by
the town historiographer, " He feared not to do what
he thought to be right."

In his turn, Rutherford, the son of Daniel, wedded
Chloe Smith, the daughter of Israel Smith, originally of
Hadley, Massachusetts, but at the time of his daughter's
marriage a principal citizen of Southwestern Vermont.
The first of the family out of England was Leftenant
Samuel Smith, who left his native town of Ipswich
in 1663 and settled in Connecticut, where he was for
twelve years a member of the Colonial Assembly.
After his removal to Hadley, where he died in **great**

esteem, he held many public trusts and was often chosen to the General Court. The family was always one of local distinction and unusual culture, and in a later generation one of Chloe's uncles went from college to preach to the Indians in Pennsylvania. He and one of his brothers, from becoming Sandemanians (" I don't know as there is any such in the country now," confesses Chloe Hayes in her diary, " nor do I know what their belief is ") became loyalists, and fled to Nova Scotia at the outbreak of the Revolution; but Chloe's father, Israel, was a staunch Whig and served under Washington, by whom he was entrusted with the arrest of certain Tories of that day, suspected of intriguing with the British in Vermont. He had lands specially granted him for his services, and he was one of three commissioners appointed to take charge of the property of refugee Tories; he was also a prominent partisan of the State of New York in her disputes with the new State of Vermont; he was employed on much public business connected with that now forgotten controversy, and he and his son-in-law both received lands from the grateful elder commonwealth.

Chloe Smith was the eldest of nine children, and, becoming the mother of eleven, lived to so great an age as to have left upon the memory of many surviv-ing grandchildren and great-grandchildren the personal impression of her strong and resolute character, and her rugged Puritan virtues, tempered and softened by æs-thetic gifts amounting almost to genius. It is to her that her posterity are fond of ascribing in vast measure whatever is best in their hereditary traits, and she certainly merits more than passing notice in the most cursory characterization of her grandson. Above all and first of all she was deeply religious, after the fashion of the days that we now think so grim, and she set her duty to God, as she knew it, before every earthly concern and affection. With a devotion almost as deep, she dedicated her days to incessant work, and her toil often saved the spirit that faltered in its religious gloom. She rose early and wrought late, as the wife of a farmer and innkeeper, and the mother of eleven children, must, and as a woman of her temperament would; and she was as intolerant of idleness in others as in herself. Even the great-grandchildren had their tasks set them in their visits to this inveterate worker, who could not rest from her labors after eighty years. She was a famous cook, and the triumphs of her skill at Thanksgivings and other sufferable holidays were no less her own pride than the solace of her guests. But she shone even more in needle-work and the now obsolete arts of the wheel and loom. "She knit more stockings, mittens, and gloves, wove more rag carpets, spun and wove more cloth, elaborated more wonderful rugs, lamp-mats, and bags, than any other woman of her generation," writes one of her grandsons; and the reminiscence of a granddaughter, at once touching and amusing, gives the color of the Puritanism which steeped in fear and misgiving the indulgence of such love of beauty as she permitted herself. " I spoke of her passion for worsted work. I have heard her say that Saturday afternoon she put it all into her work-basket, and pushed it under the bed *as far as she could ;* then, taking out her prosy knitting-work, she tried to get it all out of her mind for Sunday !" Yet she was a true artist in this passion ; her devices in worsted were her greatest delight, and she studied them from nature, going into her garden and copying the leaf or flower she meant to embroider.[1] She had an almost equal passion for flowers, for which, doubtless, she suffered the same qualms. In her old age she kept a diary, which remains to her descendants and completely reflects her stern, resolute, duteous, God-fearing, yet most tender and loving soul. In a sketch of family history, with which she prefaces her journals, she laments, with a simple pathos which no words can reproduce without the context, her possible error in setting work and duty before some other things. " My husband . . . . would sometimes say, ' The horse is standing in the barn, doing nothing. We will go and ride ; it 's no matter whether we stop anywhere.' But I would say, ' I can't leave my work.' So he would not go, or go alone. Oh, now I would say to every woman that has a good husband, Enjoy them while they are spared to you, or it will grieve you to the heart when it is too late — when all is over !" But this cry of regret, in a sorrow as keen as if the husband she had lost had been

---

[1] Most of her grandchildren inherited her artistic skill ; among her great-grandchildren are Larkin G. Mead, the sculptor, and his brother, John Mead, who died in his Junior year at Harvard, and had already given promise in art. A series of lithographs illustrating student life were published after his death.

cut off in his prime, and not in the fullness of his eighty years, is almost the sole expression of misgiving in a diary to which she confesses everything, commits every hope, fear, doubt, and imparts every mood of her soul. The faded pages, recording so vividly a type of high character which has passed away with the changing order of things, are of almost unique interest, but this is not the time or place to explore them. Work, faith, duty, self-sacrifice, continual self-abasement in the presence of the Divine perfection, are the ideal of life which they embody — the old New England ideal. It was a stern and unlovely thing often in its realization; it must have made gloomy weeks and terrible Sabbaths; but out of the true stuff it shaped character of insurpassable uprightness and strength. It is to the indomitable will, the tireless industry, the rectitude, the whole, ever-vigilant conscience, which it fostered in his austere ancestress, that this man of our choice doubtless owes the virtues on which our hopes rest. From other progenitors come the genial traits, the fine and joyous humor, the quick cordiality, the amiable presence, which a superficial observation has mistaken for the whole man ; but from her the keen sarcasm, the active intellect, the ever-present sense of duty, the immovable purpose, the practical religiousness, now no longer bound to creeds but fully surviving in the blameless and useful life.

The mother of General Hayes was Sophia Birchard, whose family had removed from Connecticut to Vermont near the close of the last century. She too has left a diary, in which we recognize many of the same religious traits so strongly marked in her mother-in-law. The circumstances of her widowhood, in the strange new country (Mrs. Chloe Hayes, on her daughter's departure for the West, speaks of her "leaving her native land," as if "the Ohio," so called in that day, were some unattainable foreign strand) whither she had followed her husband, no doubt tended to deepen the sad aspects of her faith at the expense of those happier hereditary instincts which in her brother became a strong love of art. She and her husband united with the Presbyterian Church, — the Western Puritanism, — and their children were reared in that faith, but the sole survivor of her family is not now a member of the sect in question, nor of any other, though a regular attendant, with his wife, at the Methodist services. Not many years after her husband's death, their oldest son was drowned, and there remained to the widowed mother only two of her children: a brother and sister, who grew up in a friendship most tender and affectionate on her part, and of passionate reverence and admiration on his. In a manuscript memoir of this adored sister, which must be sacred from more than a passing allusion, General Hayes recorded, shortly after her death, the simple facts of their early childhood in Delaware. It is now a pretty town of some eight thousand souls, seat of a Methodist college, and deriving its prosperity chiefly from one of the richest farming regions of Central Ohio. Its situation on the borders of the Olentangy is charmingly picturesque, and the painter

Griswold drew his first inspirations from the surpassingly lovely country in which it lies. At the early period of which the memoir treats, the land was yet new, though the pioneer period had quite passed. Mrs. Hayes dwelt in a substantial brick house in the village, and drew a large part of her income from a farm left her by her husband in the neighborhood. Besides the guardianship of her brother, she had in the care of her children and house the help of one of those faithful friends whom it is cruel to call servants, and whom in this case the children both regarded with filial affection. But life in that time and country was necessarily very simple ; this early home was in no sense an establishment; when the faithful Asenath married and set up for herself in life, the mother and the sister did all the work of the household themselves. The greatest joys of a happy childhood were the visits the brother and sister made to the farm in the sugar season, in cherry time, at cidermaking, and when the walnuts and hickory-nuts were ripe ; and its greatest cross was the want of children's books, with which the village lawyer's family was supplied. When their uncle Birchard began in business he satisfied their hearts' desire for this kind of literature, and books of a graver and maturer sort seem always to have abounded with them. They read Hume's and Smollett's English history together ; the sister of twelve years interpreted Shakespeare to the brother of ten ; they read the poetry of Mr. Thomas Moore (then so much finer and grander than now), and they paid

Sir Walter Scott the tribute of dramatizing together his " Lady of the Lake," and were duly astonished and dismayed to learn afterwards that they were not the sole inventors of the dramatization of poems, — that even their admired " Lady of the Lake" had long been upon the stage. The influence of an elder sister upon a generous and manly boy is always very great ; and it is largely to this sister's unfailing instincts and ardent enthusiasm for books that her brother owes his life-long pleasure in the best literature. She not only read with him; she studied at home the same lessons in Latin and Greek which he recited privately to a gentleman of the place ; she longed to be a boy, that she might go to college with him; in the futile way she must, so remote from all instruction, she strove to improve herself in drawing and painting. One of their first school-mas-ters was Daniel Granger, "a little, thin, wiry Yankee," of terrible presence but of good enough heart, whom " the love he bore to learning " obliged to flog boys of twice his own bulk, with furious threats of throw-ing them through the school-house walls, and of mak-ing them " dance like parched peas," — which dreadful behavior and menaces rendered " all the younger chil-dren horribly afraid of him," and perhaps did not so much advance the brother's and sister's education as their private studies and reading had done: that is frequently the result of a too athletic zeal for letters on the part of instructors. The children were not separated for any length of time until the brother's fourteenth year, when he went away to the Academy

at Norwalk, Ohio, and after that they were little together during his preparation for college in Middletown, Connecticut, and his college years at Kenyon
College, Ohio. But throughout this time they wrote
regularly to each other; she took the deepest interest
in all his studies, their devoted affection continued in
their maturer life, and when her death parted them it
left him with the sorrow of an irreparable loss.

CHAPTER II.

COLLEGE DAYS.

IT was the wish of his preceptor at Middletown that Hayes should enter Yale College. " I was educated there myself," writes the worthy Mr. Isaac Webb, in a letter to the boy's mother, most commendatory of her son, " and feel a strong attachment to the institution; and I know its advantages. . . . . He says he has perhaps given you an exaggerated idea of the *expenses* of Yale College. The necessary expenses, including everything except clothing and pocket-money, range from $150 to $200 only," — which the frugalest mother would not think very exorbitant even now. Then the writer adds testimony on a certain point in which our candidate has been painfully contrasted with the agricultural simplicity of Mr. Tilden : " I tell Rutherford that plain, decent dress is as much respected at New Haven as anywhere else ; and a dandy is as much despised, and as great an object of ridicule and contempt, as he is in Ohio. I think Rutherford is judicious in his taste, and has as little ambition to be a *fop* as any of the rest of us." That such a man should in after life abandon himself to the excesses of fashion would, if true, be a fact really regrettable,

except as the sole refuge of opponents who have found
nothing else to allege against him.

It was settled, however, that Hayes should enter college in his native State, and he was therefore examined for the Freshman class at Kenyon College, Gambier, Ohio, in November, 1838. Possibly because of
his fitness for entering an institution of severer requirements, he records his passing the examination,
and considers his Freshman studies at Kenyon with
a coolness approaching nonchalance; and his fellow-
students of that day remember his overflowing jollity
and drollery more distinctly than his ardor in study,
though his standing was always good. Even in the
serious shades of Middletown his mirthful spirit and
his love of humor bubbled over into his exercise books,
where his translations from Homer are interspersed with
mock-heroic law-pleas in Western courts, evidently tran-
scribed from newspapers, and every sort of grotesque
extravagance in prose or rhyme. The increased dig-
nity of a collegian seems to have rebuked this school-
boyish fondness for crude humor : a commonplace-
book of the most unexceptionable excerpts from classic
authors of various languages records the taste of this
time, and the reflections on abstract questions in
young Hayes's journals are commonly of that final
wisdom which the experience of mankind has taught
us to expect in the speculations of Freshmen and
Sophomores. They are good fellows, hearty, happy,
running over with pranks and jests, and joyous and
original in everything but their philosophy, which must

be forgiven them for the sake of the many people who remain Sophomores all their lives. Hayes was a boy who loved all honest, manly sports. He was a capital shot with the rifle, and he allotted a due share of his time to hunting, as well as fishing, — to which he was even more devoted, — swimming, and skating. Shortly after he went to Kenyon he records that he broke through the ice where the water was eight feet deep, and "was not scared much." His companions helped him out "without much trouble," and he adds, with something like indignant scorn, " I could have got up without any help." At Christmas time he walked forty miles home to Delaware in twelve hours, and after Christmas walked back to Gambier in four inches of snow.

There are few incidents, and none of importance, set down in these early journals. What distinguishes them from other collegian diaries, and gives them their peculiar value in any study of the man, is the evidence they afford of his life-long habit of rigid self-accountability and of close, shrewd study of character in others. At the end of his third year he puts in writing his estimate of the traits, talents, and prospects of his fellow-students; and in a diary opened at the same time he begins those searching examinations of his own motives, purposes, ideas, and aspirations without which no man can know other men. These inquiries are not made by the young fellow of nineteen in any spirit of dreamy or fond introspection ; himself interests him, of course, but he is not going to give himself any quarter on that account : he has got to stand up before his own conscience, and be judged for his suspected conceit, for his procrastinations, for his neglect of several respectable but disagreeable branches of learning, for his tendency to make game of a certain young college poet who supposes himself to look like Byron; for his fondness, in fine, for trying the edge of his wit upon all the people about him. Upon consideration he reaches the conclusion that he is not a person of genius, and that if he is to succeed he must work hard, and make the very most of the fair abilities with which he accredits himself. He has already chosen his future profession, and he is concerned about his slipshod style, and his unreadiness of speech, which will never do for an orator. He is going to look carefully to his literature, and he takes an active interest in the literary societies of the college ; about this time also he is one of " a few select friends " who found a club having for its stately object " the promotion of firm and enduring friendship among its members," and though he doubts whether the friendships thus systematically promoted will endure much beyond the graduation of the allies, he will do what he can for the club. He has to accuse himself at the mature age of nineteen of being still a boy in many things ; even after he is legally a man, he shrewdly suspects, the law will have somewhat deceived itself in regard to him. He also finds that he is painfully bashful in society, but that great relief may be found by making fun of his own embarrassments. It is a frank, simple, generous rec-

2

ord, unconscious even in its consciousness, and full
of the most charming qualities of heart and mind. Nowhere is the trace of any low ideal or sordid motive ;
nowhere the self-betrayal of an egoistic or narrow spirit.
There is uncommonly little of the rhetoric of youth-
fulness ; a good sense, as kindly-hearted as it is hard-
headed, characterizes the boy's speculations and aspirations and criticisms. The ancestral tendency to examine, consider, accuse, approve, or blame the springs of
thought and action is here in accumulated force, but
the trial goes on through all the diaries, not so much
with regard to duty to God, as in the case of the Puritan diarist, but duty to one's self and to other men ; the
stand-point is moral, not spiritual ; the aim is to be a
good man of this world. Not that the young fellow
has any doubts of the theology in which he has been
reared ; he writes with large satisfaction of how he has
labored to show a fellow-student the folly of skepticism.

As for political affairs, he does not, he affirms, take
any interest in them. He intends to be a lawyer and
to let politics alone. Yet he cannot help saying in
1841 that the Whigs " should be careful how they
hazard all by casting loose from John Tyler for a conscientious discharge of duty " in vetoing the Bank Bill.
" I was *never* more rejoiced than when it was ascertained that Harrison's election was certain. I hoped
that we should then have a stable currency of uniform
value," — a hope to which thirty-five years later he is
still loyal, — " but since Tyler has vetoed one way of
accomplishing this, I would not hesitate to try others."

A little later we find that he has " aspirations which he would not conceal from himself," and of which one may readily infer the political nature from what follows. But what follows is more important for the relation it bears to his whole career, than for the light it throws upon any part of it. " The reputation which I desire is not that momentary eminence which is gained without merit and lost without regret," he says with a collegian's swelling antithesis; and then solidly places himself in the attitude from which he has never since faltered : " *Give me the popularity that runs after, not that which is sought for.*" So early was the principle of his political life fixed and formulated! Every office that he has held has sought him; at every step of his advancement popularity, the only sort he cared to have, has followed him ; he is and has always been a leader of the people's unprompted choice.

He has much to say, from time to time, of the profession which he has determined to adopt, and he tries to measure, as a college lad may, the difficulties before him. Success will be hard, very hard, and will come only of long and patient endeavor ; he knows that, but he is not dismayed; nor when he casually listens to the arguments " of some of the first lawyers of the State," in the United States Circuit Court, is he out of heart. " They did not equal my expectations; some were indeed most excellent, yet none were so superior as to discourage one from striving to equal them." He never disparages any antagonist or difficulty, but he quietly takes account of his own powers, and decides

that he can probably stand up against the worst. That
is Rutherford Hayes at nineteen, and that is Rutherford Hayes at fifty-four.

In spite of the misgivings he has had concerning his
scholarship, and in spite of the ridicule which his diary
heaps upon college exhibitions, he is the valedictorian
of his graduating class ; and then, after a few weeks' interval, he begins his legal studies in the office of Messrs.
Sparrow and Matthews, prominent lawyers in Columbus, in the year 1842.   Thereafter his diary is largely
concerned with the progress he makes, or fails to make,
in Blackstone, Chitty, and the rest ; and with what he
is doing in German, which he has taken up with his
customary vigor.   He has to lament that, besides reading such good literature as Milton and Shakespeare, he
spends his leisure in reading a great deal of trash ; he
deplores the unprofitable fascination of the newspapers;
and he presently sets down his " rules for the month,"
which, as he never was a prig in his life, we may
safely suppose he regularly violated : —

" First, Read no newspapers.

" Second, Rise at seven and retire at ten.

" Third, Study law six hours, German two, and Ch.
two.

" Fourth, In reading ' Black.'s C'y,' to record my
difficulties."

There is not the slightest record of these difficulties.
In fact, the scene abruptly changes from Columbus, and
the next entry is made at Cambridge, in August, 1843.

CHAPTER III.

HAYES had been ten months in the office of Messrs. Sparrow and Matthews when it was decided that he should enter the Harvard Law School, where the special advantages to which he looked forward were "the instructions of those eminent jurists and teachers, Story and Greenleaf." Within the first week he has found that he likes the institution, professors, and students; he likes his room-mate, Hedges of Tiffin; he likes his associates, mostly "Buckeyes," like himself. He is in state of hopeful and joyous content with everybody and everything but himself. His irresolution, his neglect of opportunities, ought to grieve him, but he is perfectly cheerful in spite of his regrets, and he begins at once to sketch the lectures and lecturers, and first of all Judge Story and his introductory remarks. "He spoke at some length of the advantage and necessity of possessing complete control of the temper, illustrating his view with anecdotes of his own experience and observation. His manner is very pleasant, betraying great good-humor and fondness for jesting. His most important directions were: Keep a constant guard upon temper and tongue. Always have in read-

iness some of those unmeaning but respectful formula-
ries as, *per ex.*, ' The learned gentleman on the opposite
side,' ' My learned friend opposite,' etc.   When in the
library, employ yourself in reading the title-pages and
table of contents of the books of reports which it contains, and endeavor to get some notion of their relative
value.   Read Blackstone again and again — incompa-
rable for the beauty and chasteness of its style, the
amount and profundity of its learning."

 " We have no formal lectures," he writes after the end
of the first week.   " Professors Story and Greenleaf
illustrate and explain as they proceed.   Mr. G. is very
searching and logical in examination.   It is impossible
for one who has not studied the text to escape exposing his ignorance ; he keeps the subject constantly in
view, never stepping out of his way for the purpose of
introducing his own experience.   Judge Story, on the
other hand, is very general in his questions, so that persons well skilled in nods affirmative, and negative shak-
ings of the head, need never more than glance at the
text to be able to answer his interrogatories.   He is
very fond of digressions to introduce amusing anecdotes, high-wrought eulogies of the sages of the law,
and fragments of his own experience.   He is generally
very interesting, and often quite eloquent.   His manner of speaking is almost precisely like that of Corwin.
In short, as a lecturer he is a very different man from
what you would expect of an old and eminent judge ;
not but that he is great, but he is so interesting and
fond of good stories.   His amount of knowledge is

prodigious. Talk of 'many irons in the fire'! Why, he keeps up with the news of the day of all sorts, from political to Wellerisms, and new works of all sorts he reads at least enough to form an opinion of, and all the while enjoys himself with a flow of spirits equal to a school-boy in the holidays. So ho! the measures of literature are not so small after all!"

He quotes from Judge Story, whose enthusiasm for Chief Justice Marshall all the old graduates of the Harvard Law School remember, the belief that Marshall was "the growth of a century. Providence grants such men to the human family only on great occasions. . . . . Such men are found only when our need is the greatest;" and the diarist gives, from one of Judge Story's discursive addresses, a personal reminiscence which affords a glimpse, too valuable to be lost, of the noble and lofty mind whose ideals and impulses found a quick response in that of his unknown young listener :—

" When a young lawyer, I was told by a member of the bar at which I practiced, who was fifteen years my senior in the profession, that he wished to consult me in a case of conscience. Said he, ' You are a young man, and I can trust you. I want an opinion; the case is this : I am engaged in an important cause, my adversary is an obstinate, self-willed, self-sufficient man, and I have him completely in my power. I can crush his whole case ; it is in my hand, and he does not know it, does not suspect it. I can gain the case by taking advantage of this man's ignorance and overweening confi-

dence.   Now the point is, shall I do.it?' I answered,
'I think not.' 'I think not, too,' he replied. 'I have
determined to go into court to-morrow, show him his
error, and set him right.' He did it. This was forty-
five years ago, but I have never forgotten that act nor
that man. He is still living, and I have looked upon
him and his integrity as beyond all estimate. I would
trust him with untold millions, nay, with life, with
_reputation, with all that is dear."

Judge Story, indeed, seems to have had a far greater
influence than any other professor, at this time, on
the young Ohio student, who sets down so diligently
the characteristic points of the great jurist's discourses.
The two men, with all the vast disparity of their years,
traditions, opportunities, and experiences, had so many
principles in common that the younger could not but
follow the elder mind in quick and admiring sympathy.
They had the same high purposes, balanced and ordered
by the same cool good sense ; they both regarded noble
ideals of their profession in the same practical way, and
found them practicable. Whatever law was lost upon
Hayes in Story's lectures (and it is certain that he was
never the negligent student he too rigorously thinks
himself from time to time), no lesson concerning the
humanity, the grandeur, the rights and duties of the
conscientious lawyer's life, was wasted in his hearing.
He is even glad to find that his law library, which cost
$300, is sufficient for all legal necessities according to
Judge Story, who has been saying that $10,000 would
furnish such a library abundantly, and $3000 con-

veniently; and he is proud to record all the facts in
the professor's knowledge which elevate his vocation.
" Lawyers, so far as his observation extended, were
more eminent for morality and a nice sense of honor
than any other class of men. They have the most important and delicate secrets intrusted to them; they
have more power of doing mischief, and are more instrumental in healing family dissensions, neighborhood
feuds, and general ill-blood, than any other profession."
He gives a synopsis of Story's closing lecture for the
term, in which the students were urged to lay a broad
and deep foundation of legal reading; to remember
that the law was a jealous mistress, and to have nothing
to do with the charmer Politics before forty; to use
their young hopes, desires, confidence, ambition, and energy only for useful and noble ends; and were assured
that their master had a pride and interest beyond their
conception in their future success. " Pshaw!" the diarist feels constrained to add at the close of his entry,
" how my haste (indecent!) spoils the Old Man Eloquent!"

Life had opened at Cambridge in a richness and
variety which was vastly interesting to the eager,
quick-witted, whole-hearted young Westerner, and he
strove to take in as much of it as he could. The
child who had read Shakespeare at eleven with his
young sister, out in the new Ohio country, remote from
literature, the youth who had nourished his love of
letters all through his college-days upon the best En-

glish poets and essayists, the law student who takes up
German with his Blackstone and keeps his Shakespeare and Milton fresh along with his law-reports
and Chitty, and finds even his love of lighter literature
allowed and encouraged by the example of Justice
Story, now comes, at Cambridge, face to face with au-
thorship for the first time, and sees and hears the men
whose books have been his friends.   He has the great
pleasure, long denied us Cantabrigians of later times,
of hearing Mr. Longfellow lecture, now on Anglo-
Saxon literature, now on Goethe, now on other subjects in the range of his professorship, and is vastly
content with "his style, manner, and matter."   He
hears Mr. Bancroft address a Democratic meeting in
Boston; he hears President Sparks lecture on colonial
history, and the younger Dana on American loyalty;
he goes often to hear Dr. Walker, of whose sermons
he never fails to give the drift, or to testify to his
great enjoyment in them; going to the theatre for the
first time in his life, he sees Macready in Hamlet.

But in spite of many virtuous resolutions and protesta-
tions to the contrary, Hayes takes a predominant interest in politics, in public men, and public affairs.   He
fulfills all the duties of the law student; he is instant
at all lectures, and a conscientious reader of law; he
belongs to a law club and a debating club; he is busy
in the Moot Court; but he cannot keep away from the
political meetings at which Webster, and Choate, and
John Quincy Adams, and Winthrop, and Bancroft are

-speaking. He listens, sketches, and judges them all.[1] But all this interest in politics came to the end which was so tragical with the young Whigs of 1844. Their support of Henry Clay was a generous passion ; his defeat was almost a heart-break. "I would start in the world without a penny," writes Hayes on the 9th of November, "if by my sacrifice Clay could be elected President. Not that the difference to the country is likely to be great, in my opinion ; but then, to think that so good and great a man should be defeated ! Slandered as he has been, it would have been such a triumph to have elected him. But it cannot be," he continues with as hot a regret as if it were a personal sorrow. "Now I must withdraw my thoughts from party politics, and apply my whole energies to the law."

At Cambridge Hayes had been not only pursuing his law studies ; he had been keeping up his German, and reviewing his French and Greek, as well as widening his acquaintance with literature in all directions. The continual strain began to tell upon his health, although from many self-accusing entries in his journal the reader might infer that he was anything but a diligent student. He proposes, in the six weeks' vacation following the spring of 1844, to throw his books aside entirely for a season. "Since I commenced the study of the law I have taken no sufficient recreation." He

---

[1] "I heard some speakers in Marlboro' Chapel address the Whigs of Boston," he writes on one occasion. "They were good speakers, but no better than the good speakers of Ohio."

spent this vacation at Columbus, with his family, and returned again to Cambridge in the fall.   Shortly after, he graduated from the law school and went to begin the practice of his profession in Lower Sandusky, now Fremont, Ohio.   There he formed a partnership with Mr. Ralph P. Buckland, since a well-known public man in Ohio, and the colleague of Hayes in Congress. The co-partnership was of brief duration.   Hayes had not yet taken the recreation he had so long denied himself, and he began to pay the penalty of overwork. His health gave way entirely; he had even the pre-monitions of consumption, and there was nothing for it but to make an absolute change.

CHAPTER IV.

In June, 1847, Hayes had resolved to go to Mexico
and take any part in the conduct of the war that could
be assigned to the sort of detached volunteer he proposed to be. His failing health obliged him to give up
his profession, and it seems to have been his reluctance
to appear idle, rather than his desire to fight in that
unjust cause, on which he acted. "I have no views
about war other than those of the best Christians," he
writes, "and my opinion of *this* war with Mexico is
that which is common to the Whigs of the North, —
Tom Corwin and his admirers, of whom I am one."
He even went so far as to join, or take the first
steps towards joining, a company of volunteers going
from Fremont. He consented, however, at the urgence
of his friends, to take medical advice before finally deciding; his physician in Cincinnati resolutely forbade
his enterprise, and ordered him to go not South but
North. He very unwillingly gave up the design on
which he had set his mind, but he obeyed, and spent the
next summer in New England and Canada, camping
out in the mountains, and visiting all the scenes of that

family history which attached him so warmly to the East. The journey failed to restore his broken health, and he recurred to his former purpose of going South, but he had now relinquished his design of taking part in a war offensive to the political and moral ideas of a Corwin Whig.

Among the college acquaintance whose characters he had sketched in his first diary was the young Texan, Guy M. Bryan, of whom Hayes recorded, with boyish admiration and tenderness, " He is a real gentleman, holds his honor dear, respects the wishes and feelings of others, is a warm and constant friend. Has good talents. . . . . He will, I trust, figure largely in Texan history ; he is a true patriot." The two friends had never lost sight of each other ; and in the Rebellion they met in arms on opposing sides. But in 1847 their friendship was still far from this, and Hayes resolved to visit his old fellow-student in Texas, where his thousands upon thousands of acres gave a manorial vastness and state to his home. The record of this visit is a continuous story of delights of every kind : balls and parties at Bryan's house, where the troops of guests come at two o'clock in the afternoon and stay till the next day at noon ; rides to and fro over the prairies to call upon Texan ladies, who all have the brilliancy and beauty that all ladies have when one is twenty-five ; visits and parties in every direction ; shooting in a land richly stocked with every kind of game, and excursions to the wild Texan towns, picturesque with the admired disorder of life on the borders of a great war, their

streets full of backwoodsmen, soldiers, gamblers, advent-
urers, and dramatic with the occasional exploits of a
Texan statesman, who electioneers for the United
States Senate by riding through the capital and exhibit-
ing all the feats of Comanche horsemanship. These
amusements, and a long gallop through Northwestern
Texas to visit a distant estate of the Bryans', form
the perfect change and the entire rest from study
needed to accomplish the end desired, and Hayes
goes home restored to health which has never since
broken.

He had gone to Texas by way of the Mississippi and
the Gulf, and his diary abounds with sketches, slight
but graphic, of the life and character on a Western
steamboat, which he sees with Dickens-like quickness,
but paints as if merely to secure his own sense of it,
and not for any literary effect. In Texas he had less
time or disposition to write, but here, as elsewhere, he
was a keen and constant observer. One's surprise
is therefore all the greater not to find in his journal
a single expression directly referring to slavery. He
may have felt it a sort of disloyalty to his hospitable
friend to criticise the institution with which his prosperity was bound up; he is the man to have obeyed
such a chivalrous instinct; at any rate, the only passage
touching slavery, or its influence on either race, occurs
in an account of a visit to a remote planter, whom he
found " very fond of telling his own experience and
talking of his own affairs. . . . . The haughty and
imperious port of a man develops rapidly on one of

these lonely sugar plantations, where the owner rarely
meets with any except his slaves and minions."

In those reminiscences of Chloe Hayes by her grandchildren, from which we have already quoted, one of
the granddaughters says, " When grandfather would
boast that he was not shifted about with every new
tide of opinion, she would remind him that he was con-
verted in one hour from faith in colonization to rank
abolitionism. This, I think, was from reading something on the subject." Probably Hayes had received
the right principles by inheritance; he showed often
enough afterwards what his sympathies had always
been ; nevertheless it was long before he became an active political opponent of slavery, though he had been
a Whig of the Clay and Corwin antislavery school from
the first. His mind is essentially legal and conservative, and the respect for law and fidelity to the constitution and its guarantees inherent in him had been
strengthened by his admiration for Story and his opinions. He might think at least one of the constitutional
guarantees atrocious, but he did not question its existence, and it was not till slavery became openly aggressive that he began to fight it. He remained, with
whatever misgivings, a Whig till the formation of the
anti-Nebraska party upon the repeal of the Missouri
Compromise.

The first indication of what may long have been in
his thought upon the subject is in an entry in his journal in 1850. Even this is indirect, and is one of many
passages he quotes from Mrs. Adams's Letters, which
he was then reading : " Speaking of a conspiracy among

the negroes to aid the British against their masters, she says, 'I wish most sincerely there was not a slave in the Province. It always appeared a most iniquitous scheme to me to fight, ourselves, for what we are daily robbing and plundering from those who have as good a right to freedom as we have.' "

A few months later he copies into his journal, as if it had made a deep impression on him, the whole of Whittier's poem of "Ichabod," which he introduces with a significant passage : " There is much discussion in the political circles as to Mr. Webster's recent movements on the slavery question. I am one of those who admire his genius but have little confidence in his integrity. I regret that he has taken a course so contrary to that which he has hitherto pursued on this subject. I saw the following lines by Whittier in 'The New Era,' which can only refer to the godlike Daniel."

In spite of all this, however, he remained a Whig, and doubtless still hoped good things from a party that had meant so much good. The next year he meets General Scott, and in his fashion describes the person and bearing of the soldier, of whom he pronounces, at the close of his entry, " *He 'll do for President.*" Unhappily, he did not do ; but —

"God fulfills himself in many ways,"

and doubtless the Democratic success was in his providence.

On his way back to his former residence in Northern Ohio, after the Texan sojourn already mentioned,

Hayes had stopped in Cincinnati, and decided to make that city his home. He formed a law partnership, and in the leisure of waiting for business reviewed his legal studies, and read widely of the current literature, comments and criticisms on which occupy a large space in his journal. He early became a member of the Literary Club of Cincinnati, established nearly half a century ago, and including jurists and statesmen like Chase, Corwin, Ewing, Charles P. James, Hoadley, and Matthews, artists like Baird, clergymen like Conway, with journalists, and whoever else loved letters in a city always first in culture in the West. With many registered vows " to speak regularly at the club," Hayes rarely shared in its discussions, but its meetings were always times of the greatest pleasure to him, and for twelve years the club was "an important part of his life," as he wrote one "club-night" in his camp on the Kanawha, fondly recalling the club-nights of the past, and dwelling on their associations and enjoyments. He was, indeed, one of those non-literary men who take a purer and finer delight in literature than is, perhaps possible to the professional *littérateur ;* and such an event as Mr. Emerson's delivery, in Cincinnati, of a course of lectures, in 1850, finds an ampler record in his diary than any other event of the time. He heard every one of the lectures, and he reports the leading points of all in his journal. He had from his college days had a great love of metaphysics, and his reading had embraced the German as well as the English philosophy. But his favorite author (liked, however, with his own critical reservations) was Emerson, whom he read with an enjoyment equaled only by the delight he took in another supreme genius, — Hawthorne.

The general reading of this young lawyer, even after business began to accumulate on his hands, was as great as that of most men of literary life; but the difference was that he never read for a literary purpose, as men of letters do. He is as far as possible removed from the merely literary temperament. It was to find out what an author had to say, not to see how he said it, that Hayes read books, and his criticisms on what he read, though they show his sensibility to the charms of style, are always more concerned with matter than with manner. Men, character, life, are his study, not art; and it is observable that the books which most interest him are those whose substance is of vastly greater importance than their form. He delights in the novelists, and each new fiction of Hawthorne, Thackeray, Dickens, Bulwer, is a sensation marked in his diary; but when he comes casually and tardily upon the life and writings of Channing, page after page of comment and quotation manifests his intenser interest. He views the whole matter of reading from an unliterary point, yet there is a shrewd suggestiveness in many of his references to it which could not have been more aptly appreciative if he had — shall we say? — been writing a book-notice. " I am going to sip a little from Sterne's 'Tristram Shandy,'" he writes; "enough to test its qualities.

One ought to read these 'of-course' books, which every one reads, or claims to have read, as 'Don Quixote,' which *is* good, ' Gil Blas,' which *is n't* good, etc.," — a judgment which evinces a clear, if too severe, sense of the difference between the solid Spanish silver and the French plate.

He seems, like Justice Story, to have always esteemed his love of Literature a comparatively guiltless treason to that jealous mistress, the Law; it is the other siren, Politics, that he is always protesting his immovable purpose of having nothing to do with. Yet it requires no great penetration in the reader of his diary to perceive that from first to last his heart was largely given to what must in every republic occupy the natural leader of men. This shows itself in many ways, in none more distinctly than in his very resolutions against the tendency ; and the note-books, diaries, and scrap-books placed at the present writer's disposal testify that no public man now living has made a fuller, carefuller study of politics — which is but another name for contemporary history — than this man who has always refused to be a professional politician. They testify to two qualities more important to us in a President than any other except that clean conscience and high purpose which all concede to be his : a thorough knowledge of the situation and of the events tending to it during the last thirty years; and the gift, long cultivated and exercised, of judging men.

In 1852 Hayes supported Scott with the self-devotion characteristic of the Whigs in that canvas, but with no hopefulness, and with no effort to conceal from himself the fact that it was only a question between men. During the summer he made some political speeches, "neither very good nor very bad," according to his thinking, but "enough to satisfy me that with a motive in my heart and work, I could do it creditably. I would like to see General Scott elected President, but there is so little interest felt by the great body of thinking men that I shall not be surprised at his defeat. Indeed, my mind is prepared for such a result. The real grounds of difference upon impor-tant political questions no longer correspond with party lines. The progressive Whig is nearer in sentiment to the radical Democrat than the radical Democrat is to fogies of his own party, and *vice versa.*" After the election he writes, "My candidate, General Scott, is defeated by the most overwhelming vote ever recorded in this country. A good man, a kind man, a brave man, a true patriot, General Scott no doubt deserves defeat, if undue anxiety to be elected can be said to deserve such treatment;" which is not at all the fervent regret with which he had chronicled the defeat of Clay, but sufficiently well reflects the mood of most Whigs of the time.

Neither then, nor at any time, as we have already expressed, did Hayes cease to care for politics of the higher sort. But at this time his best energies were given to different work. They were devoted to saving from juridical injustice a wretched girl on trial for her life.

The Nancy Farrer case was one that in its time caused intense sensation throughout Ohio, and its event established in law the principle which medicine had long recognized, that an insane person is not morally responsible for a criminal act, although entirely sensible of the difference between right and wrong. This hapless creature, wholly in the power of the man who instigated her crimes, poisoned two families; the really responsible author of her act escaped, never to be found, and she remained, with her helpless admission of all the facts, the subject of the greatest popular excitement, and the object of a horror that prejudged her from the first, and seemed to make her fate certain.

By a chance which gave her life, and her advocate reputation and standing among the first of his profession, Hayes was appointed by the judge of the criminal court to conduct her defense. He instantly recognized his opportunity. " It is *the* criminal case of the term," he writes ; " will attract more notice than any other, and if I am well prepared will give me a better opportunity to exert and exhibit whatever pith there is in me than any case I ever appeared in ; " and he goes on at once to sketch the line of his defense, to make memoranda of what he shall read, and how he shall bring to bear on the case his " favorite notions as to the effect of original constitution and early training in forming character " and diminishing responsibility.

In Nancy Farrer, origin, training, and associations were all of the worst sort ; her father had died a sot in the hospital, her mother was insane ; with such parentage what must her life, her mind be? Once under the sway of the real murderer, who had won the wretched creature's love in order the better to enslave her will, she had no volition of her own, and she had poisoned half a score of persons without compunction or any apparent sense of the crime.

In court the popular feeling against her was heightened by the repulsive plainness and brutality of her face. Yet her advocate was firmly convinced that she was not morally a free agent, and he rested her defense entirely upon that fact; every other fact of the case he fully and freely conceded. Till that time it had been the custom of the courts to demand of the medical experts whether they believed the prisoner under trial knew right from wrong, and on the admission of such a belief jurors were charged to find according to the facts. Hayes took his stand with the humaner science upon the higher ground. He studied the whole subject of insanity in its relation to crime, and among the desultory memoranda of his diary is a passage that seems to have formed the nucleus of his argument: "Dr. Bell, of the McLean Asylum, testifies, 'I consider that insane persons *generally* know the difference between right and wrong.'" His argument made a vivid impression upon the jury and the public, and gave him name and fame at once. He seems (we infer again from the data mentioned) to have told the jury the pathetic story of Mary Lamb, impelled against her own will to slay her father and mother, and adjured them to see the parity between her case and that of the wretch before them. "Awful as are the tragedies which she has been the instrument — as I believe, the unconscious instrument — of committing, their horror sinks into insignificance when compared with the solemn and deliberate execution, by reasoning, thinking men, of such a being as she. On the subject of insanity I have asked more than is sustained by the weight of judicial opinion even in this country. But I suppose that when the facts and principles of any science come to be so well established that they are universally recognized and adopted by the most intelligent as well as the most conservative members of the profession which deals with that science, it is in strict harmony with the expansive and liberal rules of the common law that courts should also recognize and adopt those facts and principles. The calamity of insanity is one which may touch very nearly the happiness of the best of our citizens. We all know that in some of its thousand forms it has carried grief and agony unspeakable into many a happy home ; and we must all wish to see such rules in regard to it established as would satisfy an intelligent man if, instead of this friendless girl, his own sister or his own daughter were on trial. And surely to establish such rules will be a most noble achievement of that intelligence and reason which God has given to you, but denied to her whose fate is in your hands."

In spite of the sober eloquence and the logic of his plea, the girl was found guilty on the old ground that if she knew right from wrong she was answerable for her crime. He applied for a writ of error, and the question was reserved for decision in the Ohio supreme court, before which Hayes appeared in her behalf, in December, 1853, more than a year after the conviction.

He had already argued his first case in the supreme court, on a similar appeal, when an incident occurred which bears witness at once to his power and his modesty. In that day it was the custom for lawyers arguing before that court to take their places at a certain table in the centre of the court-room. It is related by one of the eye-witnesses that Hayes laid down his papers on a desk in one corner and began to speak. As he went on, the closeness and clearness of his argument fixed the attention of all. Presently one of the judges interrupted him. "Mr. Hayes," he said, "the court is desirous not to lose a word of what you are saying. Will you be kind enough to come forward to the table in the centre of the room?" The young advocate advanced and finished a plea which, though unsuccessful, was pronounced by Thomas Ewing "the best first speech" he had ever heard in the supreme court. His plea in behalf of Nancy Farrer was triumphant, and convinced the judges while it moved every listener by its profound pathos. The decision of the court established a point to which all similar defenses for insanity have since referred and must refer; the motion for a new trial was granted. But a new trial did not take place. An inquest of lunacy found Nancy Farrer of unsound mind, and she was sent to an asylum, where she died a few years after. On the day when the result of the inquest was reached, Hayes recorded the fact with modest satisfaction, and his usual temperance of statement; and we cannot better indicate the effect upon himself and his interests than by giving his own straightforward phrase: "_She will now go to a lunatic asylum, and so my first case involving life is ended successfully. It has been a pet case with me ; has caused me much anxiety, given me some prominence in my profession, and indeed was the first case which brought me practice in the city. It has turned out fortunately for me — very, and I am greatly gratified that it is so. I argued the case in December, '53, before the supreme court, at Columbus; made a successful argument. The judgment of the court below was reversed in an opinion fully sustaining my leading positions. The case is reported in 2d Ohio State Reps., Farrer versus State."

Among the notes in Hayes's diary apparently sketching the line of his argument before the supreme court, a point is made which we could not leave untouched without doing injustice to his attitude in the case; an attitude which distinguishes his defense from multiplied instances in which the plea of insanity has been made before and since. "There is no fact," he says, "more essential to crime than the possession of reason. The existence of this fact the law properly presumes. But if that presumption is denied, if there is evidence tending to overthrow it, why not apply to that evidence the same humane maxim which is extended to every other presumption of the law? The only answer I find to this inquiry is that the safety

and protection of society require this departure from
principle, that otherwise the defense of insanity would
be successfully interposed in cases where, in truth, de-
pravity, not insanity, was at the bottom of the crime.
It is needless to remark, in reply, that every presumption for the protection of innocence is liable to be used
as a shield for guilt.   The question is still to be answered, Why is the defense of insanity to be treated
as odious by the law?   Is it so peculiarly liable to
abuse that fundamental rules are to be changed to guard
society against it?   On the contrary, I believe it has
been shown by those who have investigated the subject,
the danger is in the opposite direction; that until a recent period there were ten insane, and therefore innocent, persons who suffered punishment to one criminal
who escaped on the pretext of insanity; and that now,
in view of the state of the law and the prejudices of
the community, injustice is more frequently done to the
insane accused than to the public.   I admit that cases
are occurring frequently in which this defense is set
up and the accused acquitted, when there is in truth
very little that looks like permanent and real insanity.
But what are these cases?   Are they cases of feigned
insanity, cases in which the jury are deceived, and
acquit the accused because they are deceived?   Far
from it.   They are cases in which verdicts of acquittal are rendered against the rigorous requirements of
the law, because the juries are satisfied that the acts
charged . . . . do not evince 'a heart regardless of
social duty, and fatally bent on mischief.'   They are

cases in which the accused has suffered some great wrong for which the law provides no adequate remedy." Then, citing several cases in which women have killed their seducers, he continues: "In all these cases the defense was insanity, the verdict acquittal; but the verdict would have been the same on any other plea. Nobody is deceived by the defense. Insanity is set up because under that defense more conveniently than under any other the story of the wrong suffered by the accused can be spread before the jury. The general sense of the community approves these verdicts of acquittal, because it is felt that the best person in the community might, under the same circumstances, commit the same act; because there is no other redress for such a wrong; because, finally, the slain deserves his fate. We submit that the defense of insanity is not to be regarded as odious in the law because of these cases. The same verdict would be rendered in the same cases if the plea of self-defense were set up."

His success in Nancy Farrer's case not only brought her advocate reputation and much general business, but naturally attracted to him other cases involving life. During the times of the fugitive slave cases Hayes appeared in a good many, and notably in the famous Rosetta case, when he was associated with Chief-Justice Chase and Judge Timothy Walker. The former referred to him, in a letter written a friend, as " Mr. R. B. Hayes, a young lawyer of great promise. . . . . I was most ably supported by Judge Walker, while Hayes acquitted himself with great distinction in the defense of Rosetta before Pendery."

At the close of the Nancy Farrer case, Mr. Hayes had been five years in the practice of the law at Cincinnati, at first alone and afterwards with various partners. In 1854 he went into partnership with Messrs. R. M. Corwine and W. K. Rogers, both lawyers of note ; and with the latter he formed one of those lasting friendships characteristic of a man who has had few intimacies ; his friends have been those who valued him for himself, not for what he could do for them ; and such alone know the depth and cordiality of his regard.

On the 30th of December, 1852, he was united in a marriage which has formed the crowning happiness of a singularly prosperous and happy life, with Miss Lucy Ware Webb, of Cincinnati. Her family was Kentuckian, of that sort which seems to assemble in itself whatever is fine and good in the Southern civilization, but she was herself born in Chillicothe, Ohio, where her father, Dr. James Webb, formerly of Lexington, Kentucky, had been long in practice. Her great-grandfather had, like her husband's, been an officer of the Revolution ; and other ancestors had been people of note and substance in their native State. Her father was for many years a colonizationist, but he died without carrying out his plans regarding the slaves on the family estate in Kentucky, and his children, after his death, freed them without conditions. The grateful blacks at once came to Ohio and settled as near their late owners as possible, where they long remained in the performance of all kinds of imaginary services, and the receipt of a substantial support, — as no doubt justly happened in many other cases of manumission.

Of the eight children of Governor Hayes, five are living ; the eldest is now a student of the Cambridge Law School, as his father was before him, though the younger Hayes is a graduate of Cornell.

CHAPTER V.

IT is the recollection of those who best remember Hayes as a lawyer that, though he could rise equal to occasion and make a great argument in a great case like that of Nancy Farrer, he preferably shunned forensic displays in the conduct of his cases. | He was one of those lawyers, not at all so rare as the general fame of the profession would imply, who discourage litigation in their clients.| When clients would go to law, he sought if possible to transact their business in court by the plainest statements to the jury, by quiet conferences with the judge and sober argument with the opposing counsel.

He was a successful lawyer, but the time was coming when, according to the testimony of some in his confidence, he found mere legal success unsatisfying. From 1856 to 1860 were the years when any man conscious of the power to direct and influence the popular feeling for good could hardly remain quiescent without self-reproach. Yet the temperament, the self-education, the inherited and sturdily trained character of Hayes, all forbade him to seek office. He could follow and he could lead without that, and during the days of the

Republican party's formation we find him taking part in the general movement, privately and publicly, without view to any personal result.   –

In his journals there is little record of his share in the Fremont campaign of 1856. Nevertheless he very actively engaged in the canvass, and addressed public meetings at Cincinnati and elsewhere, with constantly mounting enthusiasm for the work. Under a wood engraving of Fremont in his diary he briefly writes, "Not a good picture, but will do to indicate my politics this year: free States against new slave States;" and a little later he says, "I feel seriously the probable defeat of the cause of freedom in the approaching presidential election. Before the October elections in Pennsylvania and Indiana, I was confident Colonel Fremont would be elected. . . . . But after all, the good cause has made great progress. Antislavery sentiment has been created, and the people have been educated, to a large extent. I did hope that this election would put an end to angry discussion upon this exciting topic, by placing the general government in the right position in regard to it, and thereby securing to antislavery effort a foothold among those who have the evil in their midst. But further work is to be done, and my sense of duty determines me . . . . to aid in forming a public opinion on this subject which will ' mitigate and finally eradicate the evil.' I must study the subject, and am now beginning with Clarkson's ' History of the Abolition of the Slave Trade.'" Then follow entries showing how thoroughly he does study the subject in the whole history of the antislavery movement from its commencement in England. " How similar the struggle to that now going on here! The same arguments pro and con, the same prejudices appealed to, the same epithets of reproach, the same topics! On one side justice, humanity, freedom; on the other, prejudice, interest, selfishness, timidity, conservatism; the advocates of right called enthusiasts, fanatics, and incendiaries. . . . . Thousands whose hearts and judgment were on the side of abolition were silent because loss of trade, of practice, of social or political position, was likely to follow an open avowal of their opinions. In short, the parallel between that struggle and this is complete thus far. I shall be content if it so continue to the end. The election of day after to-morrow is the first pitched battle. However fares the cause, I am enlisted for the war."

Two years after the defeat that gave us Mr. Buchanan for President and the enemies of the nation for our masters, Hayes was chosen to his first public office. One of the Democratic members of the City Council believed too firmly in Hayes's integrity and ability to vote against him; he voted for Hayes, and by one majority the Council thus elected him City Solicitor, to fill a vacancy occasioned in that office by death. His election was received with expressions of friendly regard and with acknowledgments of his fitness for the place even by the press of the party desiring his defeat, and one newspaper recorded to his honor a fact which throws a vivid light on his character as a politician: " Though ten years in the city, Mr. Hayes was never

4

in the chamber of the City Fathers till the day after his election." "I like the looks of Hayes," said one of the councilmen on the advent of this stranger among them. " He has the appearance of a gentleman, and it is some comfort to talk to him ; " a Democrat assented that he was " very pleasant — for a Black Republican." In the following April his personal popularity was more substantially attested by his reëlection to the same office with a majority larger than that given for any other candidate on his ticket.

He discharged the duties of his office with signal ability, and with a humane sense of his obligations towards the accused, as well as society, novel in a public prosecutor, though the ends of justice were never better served. He treated the office as if it were a finality in his political career, and not merely " a stepping-stone to higher things ; " and when his term expired, in 1861, the only place he sought, the only place he would not have scorned to take, was a soldier's place in the field, wherever self-sacrifice might be most useful to his country.

He had fought the good fight for Lincoln, and he had watched with keen anxiety the effect upon the States threatening to secede. He thought, on the 9th of November, that South Carolina might go out, but that the others would draw back. " But at all events I feel as if the time had come to test this question. If the threats are meant, then it is time the Union was dissolved or the traitors crushed out. I hope Lincoln goes in." On the 4th of January, 1861, " Disunion and civil war are at hand, and yet I fear disunion and war less than compromise. We can recover from them. . . . . Crittenden's compromise! Windham, speaking of the rumor that Bonaparte was about to invade England, said, 'The danger of invasion is by no means equal to that of peace. A man may escape a pistol, however near his head, but not a dose of poison.'" "Six States have seceded," he adds on the 27th. "Let them go! If the Union is now dissolved, it does not prove that the experiment of popular government is a failure," he makes haste to say, with his abiding faith in the democratic idea. "In all the free States, and in a majority, if not in all the slaveholding States, popular government has been successful. But the experiment of uniting free States and slaveholding States in one nation is perhaps a failure. Freedom and slavery can perhaps not exist side by side under the same popular government. There probably *is* an 'irrepressible conflict' between freedom and slavery. It may as well be admitted, and our new relations formed with that as an *admitted* fact."

In April Sumter fell, and Lincoln's call for troops came, and with it came an end of all theories, all speculations beyond the question of the hour. At Cincinnati, as throughout the whole North, a wild outburst of the instantly embattled public sentiment answered the call. "I shall never forget," Hayes writes, "that Sunday evening," when the summons came. He was himself a leader of the popular enthusiasm, and wrote the resolutions of the largest of the public meetings held to welcome the summons. "Let what evils may follow, I shall not soon cease to rejoice over this event."

Then on the 15th of May, in words that seem still to burn with the sublime impulses of that hour, he records the purpose from which he never faltered throughout the four years of war that followed : " Judge Matthews [1] and I have agreed to go into the service for the war — if possible, into the same regiment. I spoke my feelings to him, which he said were his own, *that this was a just and necessary war, and that it demanded the whole power of the country;* THAT I WOULD PREFER TO GO INTO IT IF I KNEW I WAS TO BE KILLED IN THE COURSE OF IT, *rather than to live through and after it without taking any part in it.*"

[1] Afterwards a distinguished officer of the Union army, and now one of the leaders of the Ohio bar. He has been renominated for Congress by the Republicans of Hayes's former district.

CHAPTER VI.

THE EDUCATION OF A SOLDIER.

HAYES was in his thirty-ninth year when the war began. His character, rounded by time and experience, embodied the same traits and qualities which had marked it from the years when he first began to think and act for himself. Intellectually of solid rather than rapid growth, he was morally in his ripened manhood what he had always been, neither more nor less than just, honest, and sincere, a man at once circumspect and decided, self-respectfully modest, cautious, and brave, careful as he was hopeful, and sustained in whatever emergency by the indomitable good spirits with which he was born. His wide acquaintance with men had given him keener and deeper insight into himself, without changing at all the methods or the motives of his action. His conscience was, as it had always been, more alert against what he conceived his own shortcomings than those of other men, though he never failed to judge others accurately and fairly. He had worked deliberately, with brain as well as heart, into sympathy with the antislavery movement, and had taken his final stand upon the ground that slavery must not become the national principle. When he saw the defeated partisans of the system prepared to revenge themselves by the destruction of the nation which they could not rule, the logic of his whole life permitted him but one conclusion. War he abhorred, but there were worse things than war ; and when once he knew that he would rather be killed in the course of the war that was coming — that was come — than not go into it, there remained but a single question — how best to fight in it. He had made up his mind to fight. There were many semi-civil offices, honorable and necessary to the conduct of the war, which he could have performed with credit to himself and advantage to the country, but it was not his idea of duty to accept any of these. With him war meant service in the field, danger, death, if need be : the same chances that the simple country lads, springing to arms all over the country by tens of thousands, accepted, invited, in a rapture of patriotism that now seems incredible.

There came to him in this mood a colonel's commission from President Lincoln, probably at the suggestion of Secretary Chase, who knew the mettle of the man ; and the quick sense of responsibility in him to which the honor appealed gave him sudden pause.

Doubtless no one knew better than he his inherent qualities of leadership, but no one knew better his ignorance of war. In a letter to a friend, who has communicated these facts, hitherto unpublished, to the writer, he states that he has considered the case, questioned his present fitness, and decided to decline the commission : he could not take in his hands, unused to

the tremendous responsibility involved, the lives of a
thousand men, whom his inexperience might uselessly
sacrifice in the first battle, or waste through sickness
before they saw the enemy's face.   He adds, " I intend,
however, to enter the service immediately, but in some
capacity less responsible.   Meanwhile, I am studying
military tactics; have bought a copy of Hardee, and
am drilling with the club company," — a company
formed almost entirely of members of the Literary Club,
who chose him their captain.

In fine, he declined the colonelcy, and he set about
the work of studying war as he had set about
studying abolition history when he became a Republican, as he had all his life studied the thing, whatever it was, he had to do.   He mastered so much of
the science as his trained and penetrating mind, aided
by energies aroused to the last degree, enabled him
to achieve, in a period so brief, and in the beginning
of June, 1861, he accepted from Governor Dennison,
of Ohio, the majorship of the twenty-third Ohio volunteer infantry.   His superior officers were Colonel W.
S. Rosecrans, who was in civil life in Cincinnati at the
beginning of the war, and Lieutenant-Colonel Stanley
Matthews, that friend to whom Hayes had spoken his
feelings about going into the army, and who had " said
they were his own."

Two days after the acceptance of his commission,
Hayes was in camp with his regiment at Columbus,
and writing a letter of excellent content — content
with his regiment, content with the present, content

with the future of action and danger before him. "I am much happier in this business than I could be fretting away in the old office near the court house. *It is living.*"

Within ten days after going into camp with his regiment, Colonel Rosecrans was appointed a brigadier-general, and took command of the Ohio forces in West Virginia, while Colonel E. P. Scammon, an old West Pointer, succeeded him in command of the twenty-third. Hayes could not have desired a better school than camp service under another educated soldier.

No part, indeed, of his brief experience in camp at Columbus was lost upon Hayes, who would so willingly have gone through a longer training for his new duties. The anomaly of his position in some things struck him as it must have struck many other sincere and modest officers, suddenly called from civil life to the strange responsibilities of military leadership in war. "All matters of discretion, of common judgment," he writes four days after first going into camp, "I get along with easily; but I was for an instant puzzled when a captain of the twenty-fourth, of West Point education, asked me formally, as I sat in my tent, for his orders, he being officer of the day. . . . . I merely remarked that I thought of nothing requiring special attention; that if anything was wanted out of the usual routine I would let him know!"

The news of the calamitous defeat at Bull Run came with crushing effect to the novices at Camp Chase, who could hardly have been less amazed by the tranquillity

with which the intelligence was received by those of
their superiors to whom war was business. "Last
evening Adjutant-General B. took tea with Colonel S.
My mind was full of the great disaster; they talked
of school-boy times at West Point, gave the bill of fare
of different days, — beef on Sunday, fish on such a
day, etc., — with anecdotes of Billy Cozzens, the cook
and steward, never once alluding to the events just an-
nounced, of which we were all full;" and we may be
sure that Major Hayes was not the man to mention
them, with his humorous sense of the not altogether
amusing contrast. The universal, kind-hearted unfa-
miliarity with all things military in those first warlike
days found infinitely various expression, and one phase
of it was hardly more absurd than another: "The
mother of one of our officers, at Camp Chase, seeing a
boy walking upon his sentinel's beat, took pity on him,
sent him out a glass of wine and a piece of cake, with
a stool to sit on while he ate and drank. She told him
not to keep walking so, to sit down and rest; she
also advised him to resign!"

But the time for preparation was cut very short,
and on the 25th of July, some six weeks after going
into camp, the regiment, with all its imperfections on
its head, was ordered to West Virginia to help drive out
the rebel General Floyd. Raw as were the officers and
men of the twenty-third, they were probably marvels of
discipline and experience in the eyes of the loyal West
Virginians, to whose succor they had come. "Everywhere, in the cornfields and hayfields," runs one of the

major's letters home, " in the houses, in the roads, on
the hills, wherever a human being met us, we saw such
honest, spontaneous demonstrations of joy as we never
beheld elsewhere.   Old men and women, boys and children, — some fervently prayed for us, some laughed,
·and some cried; all did something that told the story.
The secret of it is, the defeat at Washington and the
departure of some thousands of three months' men of
Ohio and Indiana had led them to fear that they were
to be left to the rebels of Eastern Virginia : we were
the first three years' men filling the places of those who
had left. . . . . Our men enjoyed it beyond measure.
Many " — from the long Ohio levels bordering and
stretching back from the lake — " had never seen a
mountain ; none had ever seen such a reception. They
stood on top of the cars, and danced and shouted with
delight."   War had begun like a holiday for the brave
poor fellows who were to leave their bones on many
a battle-field and in the graves of hospital grounds and
prison-pens; but the cool-headed, steady-hearted leader
whose fame was to be forever identified with theirs
never lost sight, for a moment, of the wrinkled front
beneath the smiling mask. He shared, with a subtler
sense, their wild rapture in the beauty of the land;
letters and journals glow with his joy in the magnificent scenery, the delicious weather.; and he likes the
life in that first camp at Weston immensely. " The
effect is curious of this fine mountain air ; everybody
complains of heat, but everybody is in a laughing humor ; " " the soldiers fare very well here, and stand in

little need of sympathy, but when I have an opportunity to smooth matters for them, I try to do it, always
remembering how you " — the reader will know to
whom this must have been addressed — " would wish
it done." There is little or no sickness in camp, the
men are gay and full of high 'hopes; but the major
is not so gay for them as he feigns, and in a few days
he has to write home of the first blood they have shed,
— in a fight with guerrillas, who infest the beautiful
hills, and "rob and murder the Union men" in the
charming valleys. "Nevertheless, these marchings and
campings in the hills of Western Virginia will always
be among the pleasantest things I can remember. I
know we are in frequent perils, that we may never
return, and all that, but the feeling. that I am where I
ought to be is a full compensation for all that is sin-
ister, leaving me free to enjoy as if on a pleasure
tour." In the mean time he is interested, as usual, by
the character about him, in the officers and men, and
in the local life: in a settlement of Yankees, who had
come to Weston forty years before, and had kept
intact the thrift, morality, and loyalty of their native
Massachusetts; in the admirable stuff among the native
Union men; in the simple-heartedness and good nature among the better class of the Floyd soldiers taken
prisoners, "friendly, civil fellows, whom it seems so
absurd to be fighting;" in the cowardice, cunning, and
laziness of the baser sort of rebels, whose "highest ambition is to shoot a Yankee from some place of safety."

The little army of Western Virginia had on the

1st of September, after a succession of slight brushes
with the enemy, marched upon Carnifex Ferry, where
Floyd's force was strongly posted,[1] and on the evening
of the 10th attacked him. The same night Floyd
abandoned his post and fled with all his army across
Gauley River, sharply pursued, in spite of heavy rains
rendering pursuit almost impossible, by the Union
troops, who took a large number of the rebels. Nothing but the approach of night saved Floyd's army
from capture, and his rout left all Western Virginia
in the possession of our troops.

In this first affair Major Hayes was ordered, half an
hour after the attack began, to follow an aid of Rosecrans, and form with four companies of the twenty-third
the extreme left of the attacking force. Pushing on
over a hill and through a cornfield they arrived within
three quarters of a mile of the enemy's work, when the
aid took a friendly leave of them. He had no orders to
give Major Hayes ; Major Hayes was an officer, and
would know what to do in circumstances and localities
of which the aid frankly confessed himself entirely ig-
norant. The situation might have been embarrassing;
Major Hayes simplified it in the only possible way by
leading his men forward against the enemy. They had
a tough scramble through the dense laurel thickets of the
hillside, and the major reached the bottom at the head

---

[1] For a clear and succinct history of the twenty-third Ohio, see Mr.
Whitelaw Reid's admirable work on "Ohio in the War," — a really
monumental work which is yet to be fully appreciated. The writer
gladly acknowledges his obligations to Mr. Reid's volumes for the outline of the present sketch of General Hayes's career.

of four or five men. As soon as others could join him, he formed his little force and followed his skirmishing line in the enemy's direction, arriving in time, near the close of the fight, to be exposed to the rebels' fire. Some of the men were wounded; it had been growing dark; the firing now ceased, and the major's command made its way back to the rest of the twenty-third through confused and broken regiments and companies straggling about over the field, and talking of the slaughter, — thirteen killed and some seventy wounded, as it afterwards appeared. At dawn loud shouts proclaimed the flight of the enemy from his works, and the pursuit began.

The victory was greater than the battle, and Major Hayes's part, useful and difficult as it was, gave him but a slight foretaste of war. What was better, it enabled him to test himself in doing a duty which he had to discover for himself; and holding himself coolly in hand, as he has always done in every crisis of life, he perceived that he went into action with the same sensations that he commonly experienced on entering upon an exciting law case. With him, too, war had become business. The affair also taught our troops self-reliance, and showed them that such at least of the enemy as were under Floyd were no match for them, even with the odds in the rebels' favor.

The twenty-third went into camp on New River, after its return from the pursuit, and there lost many by sickness. At this time Major Hayes was detached from the regiment, and ordered to join General Rose-

crans at his head-quarters as judge-advocate. The
appointment was by no means to the taste of a man
who had gone into the war to fight. He submitted
with reluctance, comforting himself with the hope of
release after a few weeks, but going diligently about
the duties of his office, reducing them to system, keeping a record of cases, and studying the whole business
as was his wont with whatever he took hold of. Six
weeks later he was, to his high satisfaction, relieved
from the office, in which he had in the mean time done
most acceptable service, and allowed to rejoin his regiment in Camp Ewing, on New River.

Important changes had recently taken place in it.
Lieutenant-Colonel Matthews had been appointed to
the command of another regiment, and Hayes succeeded
to the vacancy, his own place being filled by another
brave soldier, now General J. M. Comly, who had re-
signed the lieutenant-colonelcy of a regiment in Camp
Chase and taken the majorship of the twenty-third,
that he might get at once into active service. His
fortunes were thereafter closely united with those of
Hayes, and when the latter became brigadier-general,
Major Comly succeeded him in command of the twenty-third, and was himself brevetted brigadier-general
at the close of the war, for his able and gallant soldiership.

The rest of the winter was spent at Camp Ewing
and the subsequent camp of the regiment at Fayetteville, in duties whose faithful performance endeared
Colonel Hayes to his men as much as his bravery in

battle. He was very diligent in drill and parade, but he was as constant in his attention to the comfort of the men as to their discipline. That humane and unselfish heart, to which all suffering and helplessness irresistibly appealed, was sensitively alive to the rights of the brave fellows — who were in some sort his children — to everything that could be done for their welfare. At the same time he wrote home indignant denunciations of the exaggerated reports of suffering in the army. " I am satisfied that our army is better fed, better clad, and better sheltered than any other army in the world. . . . . I am now dressed as a private, and I am well dressed ; I live habitually on soldier's rations, and I live well. . . . . It is the poor families at home, not the soldiers, who can justly claim sympathy. I except, of course, the regiments which have bad officers. . . . . Government is sending enough, if colonels would only do their part. . . . . We have sickness, which is bad enough, but it is due to causes inseparable from our condition." He early taught himself to relieve the needless ills of the soldiers' condition, and he was consequently successful in teaching them to bear those which could not be helped. The only complaint which escapes him on his own account is amusingly characteristic : " If J—— comes, let him get an assortment of late papers, ' Harpers,' ' Atlantics,' etc., and keep them till he gets to our camp. We are the outermost camp, and people are coaxed out of their literature before they get to us."

Hayes was never one of the Union soldiers who cou-

ceived it his business to enforce the fugitive slave law
in favor of the rebels; his mind was clear in regard to
the slavery question from the start. No contrabands go
back to their masters from the army of West Virginia,
he is glad to know; and again and again his letters
and journals bear witness to his conviction that "the
deadliest enemy the Union has is slavery, — in fact, its
only enemy, — and that to strike at slavery is to strike
at the life of the rebellion." He recurs from time to
time, with the anxiety of a man used to watch public
affairs, to the changing attitude of the government in
respect to the institution, and hails with deep satisfaction, as a step towards the final result, Lincoln's recommendation that the federal aid be pledged to States
taking measures for gradual emancipation. But for the
most part his mind is on the business in hand, requiring
from day to day a more vigilant devotion, and soon to
absorb every energy.

Early in November the twenty-third left Camp Ewing
to join another movement against Floyd, returning from
which they went into winter quarters at Fayetteville.
Under command of Lieutenant-Colonel Hayes they
quitted these quarters on the 17th of April, and led the
advance upon the enemy, who evacuated Princeton before them, but attacked the twenty-third with four regiments on the 8th, and forced it to retire to East River.
It fell back in good order, and after great sufferings and
privations, its supplies having been cut off, abandoned
Princeton, and, returning to Flat Top Mountain, remained in camp there till the 13th of July. On the

15th of August it was ordered from its next station, at Green Meadows, to Camp Piatt on the Great Kanawha, and made the march of one hundred miles in three days. Embarking in transports for Parkersburg, the regiment there took the cars for Washington, joined McClellan's force in driving the Confederates from Frederick City, reached Middletown on the 13th of September, and took part in the battles of South Mountain and Antietam.

The battle of South Mountain was fought on the day after the arrival of the twenty-third in Middletown, and three days before the battle of Antietam. It began early on a lovely Sunday of September, with the advance of Lieutenant-Colonel Hayes's command. McClellan's army with Burnside in front was pressing up the mountain by the National Road. General Cox's division of Ohio men led General Burnside's corps, and the twenty-third formed the van of that division. At seven o'clock, Hayes was ordered to take one of the mountain paths and get round the right of the rebels, who were believed to be posted there with two guns, and he started up the hill on this by-road, throwing out one company as skirmishers and two others as flankers. At nine o'clock he drove in a rebel picket; he pushed forward and in a few minutes saw the rebels coming down upon him in strong force from a hill in front. These men were, as he afterwards learned, two regiments, the twelfth South Carolina and twenty-third North Carolina, who were thus opposed to the twelfth and twenty-third Ohio. Hayes hurriedly formed his men in the woods and charged over rocks and broken ground and through underbrush, while the enemy poured in a heavy fire at short range; but he succeeded in driving them, after a fierce engagement, out of the woods into an open field near the top of the hill. His men stopped at a fence in the border of the woods and opened a brisk fire on the enemy, who took shelter behind the stone walls and fences along the crest of the hill, and returned the fire of the Ohioans across the field. At this juncture Lieutenant-Colonel Hayes, urging his men to charge the Carolinians (who were supported by a large rebel force with artillery, probably the two pieces Hayes had been sent to take), left the shelter of the woods. As he gave the command, a minie ball struck him with stunning, shattering force in the left arm, above the elbow, crushing the bone to fragments and carrying part of it completely away. He called to a soldier near him to tie his handkerchief above the wound, fearing an artery might have been severed. Then, turning suddenly faint, he fell. His men pressed beyond him, and when he regained consciousness he found himself some twenty feet in their rear, under a heavy fire, with the balls pelting the earth all about him. He listened anxiously, as he lay there, for the approach of reënforcements, and directed the movements of his men. Once, seeing what appeared to him a false movement on their part, he struggled to his feet and began to countermand it, when he was again overcome by weakness and sank down, where he remained for twenty minutes exposed to the enemy's fire, while the wounded men staggered past him or were carried to the rear. His men were gradually forced back to cover, and he was left lying between them and the rebels. He thought that they were retreating, and called out, " Hallo, twenty-third men ! are you going to leave your colonel here for the enemy? " Half a dozen good fellows sprang from the woods, and the enemy, who had suspended their fire for a moment, opened on them, and the battle began to rage again as hotly as ever. Hayes ordered the men back, and then Lieutenant Jackson came to him and insisted on taking him out of range of the fire. The command now fell to Major Comly, who led the regiment with his accustomed bravery through the rest of the day. Reënforcements coming up at last, the twenty-third again charged the enemy and drove them from the hill into the woods beyond, killing large numbers with the bayonet. The regiment then rejoined its division, making three successful bayonet charges during the fight, and losing nearly two hundred men. "The colors of the regiment were riddled," says Mr. Reid, " and the blue field almost completely carried away by shells and bullets."

Lieutenant Jackson led his colonel beyond the enemy's fire, and Hayes then growing faint from his wound, the lieutenant left him behind a log, with a canteen of water, and in company with many wounded of both sides. The man nearest him was a Confederate, and the two fell into talk of that friendliness which seems to have always been the natural condition of the men of both armies when they were not actually killing each other. " What regiment do you belong to, and where are you from ? " asked the Northerner ; and

the Southerner answered that he was major of a North
Carolina regiment. " Well, you came a long way to
fight us." " Where are you from?" asked the major
in his turn. "I am from Ohio." " Well, *you* came a
good ways to fight *us*," rejoined the major; and the
enemies " talked on in that pleasant, friendly way, neither of us at that time suffering much." The Southerner told the Northerner that he had been a Union
man, and saw no reason for secession, but went out with
his section.

The firing again died away; Lieutenant Jackson returned and led his colonel to the regimental surgeon,
who dressed his wound. Hayes then walked half a
mile to a point where he found an ambulance, and
was carried to Middletown. Here he remained, restive
and helpless, while the army marched by under the
windows of the house where he lay. He heard them
going all night long and all day long, the men sing-
ing as they marched; and he gained what small ease
he could, as he impatiently listened afterwards to the
sounds of the battle of Antietam, by hiring two boys
to stand at the window and describe the men who rode
by from the field, striving to guess from this report of
their looks how the battle was going.

A curious circumstance in regard to Hayes at the
battle of South Mountain is the fact that at the time
he received his wound he was not in the pay or service
of the United States. He had been appointed colonel
of the seventy-ninth Ohio, and had been mustered out
as lieutenant-colonel of the twenty-third without his

knowledge. His wound prevented his taking command of his new regiment, and on the 30th of November he rejoined, as colonel, the twenty-third, Colonel Scammon having been appointed a brigadier-general, and Major Comly having received the recognition his conduct merited, in promotion to the lieutenant-colonelcy.

During his convalescence in Ohio, Colonel Hayes, resisting the friends who thought he had "had his share" and counseled him to remain out of the service, gladly returned to the command of his old regiment. Of his affectionate pride in it his letters and journals give constant proof, and the men returned his regard with equal devotion.

While yet in West Virginia, the regiment was ordered against a rebel force near Princeton, and, the 1st of May, seventy-five of them were attacked by three hundred cavalry and guerrillas, and lost a third of their number in killed and wounded; but they beat the enemy, who fled, leaving his wounded with them. "As I rode up they saluted with a present arms; several were bloody with wounds as they stood in their places; one boy limped to his post who had been hit three times. As I looked at the glow of pride on their faces my heart choked me; I could n't speak; but a boy said, '*All right, colonel; we know what you mean!*'"

Their colonel was always writing home praises of their prowess or their discipline, and his letters abound in their jokes. They were humorists in their way, as all unspoiled Americans are, and in their march through

a friendly section of Maryland, where the admiring
women, children, and negroes called out from every
house to know what troops they were, their drollery
bubbled out in such answers as "The twenty-third
Utah," "The twenty-third Bushwhackers," "Drafted
Men," "Home Guards," "Peace Men," "The Lost
Tribes," and so forth. It was men of the Kanawha
division who, being at home on furlough, took from its
bearer and trampled under foot a transparency in a
Democratic procession — a brutal and shameless cari-
cature of their leader dodging the bullets they had seen
him brave; and Hayes had more than once been as quick
in the defense of their honor. One evening a corps
commander dashed furiously into their camp, where he
found them taking straw from a stack for bedding, and,
assailing them in the atrocious language which even a
brave and skillful general could suffer himself to use towards men as good as he, demanded to see their colonel. Lieutenant-Colonel Hayes presented himself and
respectfully but firmly defended them, saying that they
had always taken forage and other necessaries, and that
in a friendly country they were ready to pay for them.
Then after some further angry words from the general
he added, "I trust our generals will exhibit the same
energy in dealing with their foes that they do in the
treatment of their friends." As the general rode away
the men cheered their colonel, — a little rueful, perhaps, about his sarcasm, but glad to have defended the
brave fellows unjustly assailed and forbidden to speak
for themselves.

CHAPTER VII.

EARLY in October of 1862, the twenty-third was ordered with the rest of the Kanawha division to return to West Virginia, and went into winter quarters near the falls of the Great Kanawha. Here, on the 30th of November, a party of officers welcomed back their colonel, and they had a jovial meeting, "fighting over again the battle of South Mountain, with many anecdotes, much laughter and enjoyment."

The colonel had come home to them reëstablished in health from the general effect of his wound,[1] but his arm was still very weak, and easily hurt ; he could not raise his hand above his head. With any severe exertion, the whole limb was very painful. Under the circumstances, Lieutenant-Colonel Comly and Major McIlrath relieved him of drill duty, and he interested himself chiefly in the superintendence of the sanitary arrangements of the camp — matters which he always looked to personally if possible. The men had built them-

---

[1] He had had the best of nursing in the family of Mr. Jacob Rudy at Middletown, before his wife could join him, and her coming only intensified the care he received. Three weeks after he was shot he walked over the battle-field with Mrs. Hayes on his fortieth birthday.

selves cabins of planks and logs, and prepared to pass
the winter in as much comfort as can fall to the soldier's lot.   They took peculiar pride in fitting up the
colonel's quarters, and when, late in January, his wife
came with her three boys to visit him, it was matter of
rejoicing for the whole regiment.   Other ladies joined
their husbands in camp, and the winter passed gayly
in such amusements as the life afforded: rides, fishing,
boating, and pleasure excursions of every sort.   The
little ones became the children of the regiment so far as
the soldier's love could adopt them; with the colonel's
wife and boys in camp each good fellow was nearer the
wife and boys so far away at home.

But these gentle women could not suffer their sojourn in camp to be merely a pleasure to themselves,
and Mrs. Hayes, who remained longest, had the privilege
of doing the most kindness to the men so proud of her
presence.   "His wife is a noble woman" (we are
letting one of the soldiers speak for himself); "there
was not a morning that she omitted going through
the hospital, and she did everything she could for the
sick and wounded."   "Into our midst," writes another,
"sitting at our camp fires, putting new heart into
many a homesick boy, banishing the fever from many
a bronzed cheek with her gentle touch, came this fair
lady and her boys.   We named our camp, in her honor,
Camp Lucy Hayes, and not a man in all those thousands, but would have risked his life for her."

Mrs. Hayes's visit ended in March.   A second visit
which she paid her husband in June, when his regiment

was encamped at Charlestown, Virginia, was saddened by the death of their youngest boy whom she had brought with her. From this sorrow Colonel Hayes was shortly summoned to take part in the pursuit and capture of John Morgan, after his famous raid through Ohio.

On the 2d of July Morgan crossed the Cumberland at Burkesville with twenty-four hundred and sixty men, and struck through the State of Kentucky to the Ohio River. In five days he reached the river, sixty miles below Louisville, seized two steamers in which he set his men across, and then resumed his rapid ride, pushing through Southern Indiana towards Cincinnati. He rode fifty and sixty miles a day, leaving bridges burnt, telegraph wires cut, and general consternation behind him. By the 12th it was known that he was aiming at Cincinnati, where navigation and business were stopped and martial law proclaimed. The governor called out the militia of the southern part of the State, but Morgan came so swiftly and so secretly that, when on the morning of the 14th he passed through the suburbs of the city, he met not so much as a hostile picket, and by four o'clock in the afternoon he had reached a point twenty-eight miles east of Cincinnati, having ridden ninety-eight miles in thirty-five hours. Desertions had reduced his numbers to two thousand, and any military object which the expedition might have had was defeated by the insubordination of his followers, who abandoned themselves to plundering. But the people made all haste to hide their horses, cattle, and silver, and Morgan's men seem to have been chiefly terrible to

shops abounding in calicoes. With the best disposition in the world to steal everything, they had no time
for research. Fifty thousand militia had taken the
field against them, but having fully supplied themselves
with dress goods the raiders dashed on, and outrode or
outgeneraled the militia, and reached the Ohio River at
Pomeroy on the 19th, having met with very little fighting in their course, and only such molestation as independent sharp-shooters or small bodies of militia could
offer them in passing. But by this time a body of the
regular cavalry, under Judah, and a division of the militia were close upon him, and at Pomeroy he first en-
countered a disciplined force.

On the 16th of July, Colonel Hayes heard of Morgan's presence in Ohio and prepared to head him off.
He ordered the steamboats lying at Charleston to be
sent on to Luke Creek on the Kanawha, the highest
point to which boats go in that river, and prevailed on
his commanding officer to allow him to take men for
his enterprise. He chose two regiments and a section of
artillery, and embarking his force, reached Gallipolis,
Ohio, on the 18th. On the 19th, Sunday, he had pushed
on to Pomeroy, where he found the militia in position,
waiting for Morgan, who came about noon from Buffing-
ton Island. Hayes's force went out to meet him, and
after a slight skirmish Morgan fled, pursued by the
twenty-third. The next morning at daylight he was
attacked by Judah's cavalry and the gunboats, together
with the force under Hayes, and after a brief engagement entirely routed. More than half his command

was captured, and, pursued and attacked in all his doublings and turnings, he shortly afterwards surrendered with the remnant of his men, and was sent to the Ohio penitentiary.

Colonel Hayes's letters describe his share in Morgan's discomfiture as "the liveliest and jolliest little campaign we ever had," — "a jolly time." "The cavalry, gunboats, militia, and our infantry, each claim the victory as their peculiar property. The truth is, all were essential parties to the success." This is the verdict of a just man who could always afford to be generous, and we can easily render full credit to the other forces engaged in Morgan's defeat (he was finally run down by a body of Michigan cavalry), while recognizing the military insight and the personal vigor and decision with which Hayes planned his share of the movement against Morgan, and was enabled first of all to strike him.

CHAPTER VIII.

CLOYD MOUNTAIN AND WINCHESTER.

THE twenty-third returned, with the rest of Hayes's command, to Charleston, where it lay in camp till April 29, 1864. The interval was a season of preparation and expectation for various services; and in the mean time Colonel Hayes was more than once called upon to consider the subject of promotion for himself, which could have been easily secured if he had been more ambitious to advance his own interests than to do his duty in the station where he found himself. His feeling seems to have been that he would "rather be one of the good colonels than one of the poor generals." He knew very well that the colonel of a regiment had one of the most agreeable positions in the service, and one of the most useful, and he liked a good colonel's ability to make a good regiment. Only two things made him anxious : that he might have a stupid brigadier put over him, or that through losses his regiment might disappear or be consolidated with others and that thus he might lose his colonelcy. But he was not very anxious. He did not seek promotion, and as usual promotion was seeking him.

When the twenty-third finally moved in April, it

was to join the forces under General Crook in a raid on the Virginia and Tennessee Railroad. "This expedition," says the writer in "Ohio in the War," "was something worthy of their mettle. Their long inaction had not hardened their sinews or made them impervious to fatigue. But, as was their custom, the rank and file of the twenty-third entered into the expedition with cheerfulness and a determination if possible to make it signally successful. Without detailing their daily marches, it is sufficient to say that the regiment toiled on over the rugged mountains, up ravines and through the dense woods, meeting with snows and rain in sufficient volume to appal the stoutest hearts; but they toiled patiently, occasionally brushing the enemy out of their way until, on the 9th of May, 1864, the Battle of Cloyd Mountain was fought."

In this affair Colonel Hayes commanded a brigade, including of course his own regiment; the other regiments and parts of regiments were mainly Ohio troops, used to service under him, and eager as the twenty-third for the fight. Apparently the great object of the expedition was to destroy the Virginia and Tennessee Railroad bridge on New River, which would cut the great line of communications between Richmond and the Southwest; and General Crook, whom the Sioux now call the Gray Fox, brought his peculiar shrewdness to the undertaking. As he marched up the Kanawha he sent his music with one regiment towards Leesburg in the direction of Richmond, while he made his way in an entirely different direction toward the New River bridge, ordering the bands thus detached to play as if the whole army were with them. The first feat of the expedition was the bloodless capture of Fort Breckenridge, out of which the enemy fled at the approach of Crook's force. On the parapet of this fort the rebels had handsomely carved the words Fort Breckenridge, for which the Ohio men immediately substituted Fort Crook. When too late, the enemy found out their mistake in abandoning the fort and hurried back, and gathered finally with a considerable force under General Jenkins, formerly a Democratic member of Congress. Jenkins placed his army across the track of Crook's men fifty miles southward, where they had to traverse a high mountain ridge. At this point there was a good road, a creek, and a broad, beautiful meadow stretching before it. The ridge was called Cloyd Mountain, and here the enemy intrenched themselves. Crook's men arrived at about eleven o'clock on the 9th, and as soon as they came within cannon shot the enemy opened fire upon them, and they formed in the woods on either side of the road. It was plain that Jenkins was very strongly fortified, and that his position could not be carried without severe fighting. An attack was made and repulsed, when General Crook came to Colonel Hayes and ordered him with his brigade and the brigade on its right to cross the meadow and charge up the hill upon the batteries, adding that he would himself accompany him. The two brigades formed in the borders of the woods and marched out in perfect line. They were fresh from camp, where they had been

thoroughly drilled and could march well. The enemy's
fire opened heavily, but not a great number of men
fell. The rest quickened their pace, keeping their line
good until they got to the edge of the woods. They
could not yet see the fortification, which was on a
woody hill, and at the foot of the hill was the creek, not
very wide or deep, which had remained equally unseen.
They dashed through the creek, the bed of which was
some four feet below the level of the meadow, and
started up the hill at a point so steep that the curva-
ture of the ground protected them from the enemy's
fire. Here they stopped to take breath and shake the
water out of their boots, and then they charged up the
hill again. As they passed the protecting curve, they
faced a murderous fire. Men and officers fell in awful slaughter on all sides. The whole line seemed to
go down, but the men who were not hit did not stop.
There was no straggling; the men responded cheerfully to the encouragement of their officers, and were
soon at the fort. It was an earthwork hastily thrown
up and strengthened with fence-rails thrust endwise
into it and through it, forming an embankment extremely difficult to surmount, and held by the enemy
in perfect confidence. But Hayes's men scrambled
over at once, the first being brave Private Kosht, a boy
of eighteen, a new recruit, who sprang from the line
with a shout, and hung his hat on the muzzle of a cannon. The fight in the fort lasted only ten minutes,
but it was desperate while it lasted, a wild hand-to-hand
combat, which ended by the Ohioans beating the rebels

out and taking prisoners all who could not run away.
Then they pushed swiftly after the fugitives to keep
them from re-forming, which they attempted at a
second ridge of the mountain.   The rebels yielded to
the second charge here made upon them, but formed
again, reënforced by a body of the men who had been
raiding under Morgan, and had lived to fight another
day by taking care of themselves in time.   They were
promptly broken to pieces by the third terrific charge,
and the fight was over.   Our men hurried on eight miles
further to Dublin Depot, on the railroad line, where
they burned the bridge aimed at, and destroyed the
road, rails, ties, and bed, for several miles, so that the
rebels were unable to use the line for six weeks.

In a letter written home ten days later, Colonel
Hayes says: "This is the most completely successful
and by all odds the pleasantest campaign I have ever had.
Now it is over," he adds, — he was not only a bayonet that thought, but a bayonet that pitied, and he never
loved war but as a means, — "I hardly know what I
would change in it, *except to restore life and limb to the
killed and wounded.*"   Then a sentence that follows is
peculiarly like Hayes in its manly modesty: "My command in battles and on the march behaved to my entire
satisfaction ; none did, none could have done better.
We had a most conspicuous part in the battle of Cloyd's
Mountain, *and were so lucky!*"   Lucky, indeed, as
true and valiant men are in whatever they set their
hands to, and lucky as Hayes has always been, through
being simply worthy and capable of everything he has
undertaken in his most prosperous career.

Crook's army proceeded on its course after destroying the New River bridge, and, with some slight encounters with the enemy, who constantly harassed our men on their march over roads rendered almost impassable by the heavy rains, arrived at Staunton on the 8th of June, where Hayes's brigade joined General Hunter's command. On this march the army was encumbered by multitudes of contrabands, men, women, and children, and suffered from privation amounting almost to famine.

On the 11th, the corps arrived before Lexington, which was taken after an artillery and sharp-shooter fight of three hours. Hayes's brigade had the advance, · and nearly all the casualties fell to him. His brigade had now become as dear to him as his own regiment, and he was proud of it as one of the best in the army. On the 14th he led it within two miles of Lynchburg, and drove a body of the·enemy as many miles up the Virginia and Tennessee Railroad. The army camped for the night near Lynchburg, and so near a body of rebels, in the dark, that the men of both sides took rails from the same fence for their fires.

On the 18th, Crook's command set out to cross the James, and take Lynchburg in the rear, when news came that the enemy, heavily reënforced, was about to attack Hunter's centre. Crook's force met and repulsed the attack, a very sharp one, and the same evening reenforcements for the enemy continuing to pour in from Richmond, the retreat of our side began. "The men," says Mr. Reid, "had had no sleep for two days and nights, and scarcely anything to eat. In this condition

they marched, frequently falling down asleep in the
road, it being with great difficulty that they could be
kept on their feet." The whole retreat, which continued
till Charleston was reached on the 1st of July, was
attended with immense suffering, suffering borne, as the
journal of one of the officers testifies, with the most
heroic patience. "The men had nothing to eat, the
trains having been sent in advance. It is almost incredible that men should have been able to endure so
much, but they never faltered, and not a murmur escaped them. Often they would drop out silently, ex-
hausted, but not a word of complaint was spoken."
During whole days they pushed on, skirmishing heavily
with the enemy, who hung upon their rear, and neither
eating nor sleeping. At last, "on the 27th, a supply
train was met on Big Sewell Mountain, — men all
crazy, — stopped and· ate, marched and ate, camped
about dark, *and ate all night.*"

Of this expedition and retreat, Colonel Hayes himself wrote in one of his letters home, " We have had
altogether the severest work I have yet known in the
war. We have marched almost continually for two
months, fighting often, with insufficient food and sleep;
crossed the three ranges of the Alleghanies four times,
the ranges of the Blue Ridge twice; marched several
times all day and all night without sleeping. We all
believe in our general [Crook]. He is a considerate,
humane man, a thorough soldier and disciplinarian."

Remaining at Charleston till the 10th, Crook's command was ordered east to meet Early, then invading

Maryland and Pennsylvania. On the 18th, Hayes's brigade was sent, without cavalry and with but two sections of a howitzer battery, to attack more than twenty thousand of Early's men some ten miles beyond Harper's Ferry. They were surrounded by two divisions of rebel cavalry, but cut their way through and got safely back to camp, joining Crook at Winchester on the 22d. Here, two days afterwards, Hayes shared in the first defeat he had known. His brigade was sent out to meet what was supposed to be a reconnoissance in force on the part of the enemy, with orders to join his right to that of another brigade, and charge with it. This brigade was commanded by Colonel Mulligan. Hayes rode out to the right of his line in an open valley, and made himself known to Mulligan, whose orders he found were to fight with him and keep the two lines together; also to attack whatever was in front. These coincided with Hayes's instructions, and the brigade prepared to attack. Two lines of rebels, fighting as skirmishers, were alone visible, but there were reports of the enemy on the hills to the right and left, inclosing the valley in which the brigades were drawn up. A little closer inspection now developed the enemy on these hills in immense force. The two colonels perceived that they were in a trap, but they pushed forward according to orders, and in five minutes Colonel Mulligan fell, pierced with five balls. The enemy came to meet the attack, and closing upon our vastly inferior force, easily drove it before them, Hayes's brigade retreating till it struck a rough, wooded hill. Here he formed his men, Colonel Comly of the twenty-third being wounded at this point, and held the hill while the enemy pressed him hard on all sides. His resistance threw them into some confusion. He cleared his line of them, and continued his retreat in good order, although attacked continually for twelve miles. When the enemy pressed his men too hard, they turned and beat them back, and so made good their escape. They presently joined Crook's force, and the retreat continued till midnight, when the enemy ceased to pursue. From the peculiar nature of the ground, and the position of the opposing forces, Hayes was probably then in greater danger than he had ever been before, all the officers. being exposed to the fire of the enemy's sharp-shooters, who could easily pick them off at short range; but he lived to retrieve the disastrous fortunes of that day on the same field a little later. His horse was shot under him, and he was struck in the shoulder by a spent ball. His brigade, after being in the hottest of the fight, was in condition to cover the retreat as rear guard, which it did successfully for twenty-four hours. ' "We are queer beings," he writes from his camp near Sharpsburg, two days after; "the camp is now alive with laughter and good feeling — more so than usual — the recoil after so much toil and anxiety."

For almost a month Hayes's brigade was engaged in daily skirmishing, with varying fortune, up and down the Shenandoah Valley, till at Halltown, on the 23d of August, he repulsed an attack, dashing out and picking up "a small South Carolina regiment entire." "This charge was brilliantly executed," says Mr. Reid, "and excited astonishment among the rebel prisoners," who expressed their surprise in the characteristic demand, "Who the —— are you 'uns?"

On the evening of the 3d of September, at Berryville, an engagement of uncommon fierceness took place between the South Carolina and Mississippi division under Kershaw and the Kanawha division, Hayes's brigade sustaining the hardest of it. At ten o'clock the fighting ceased without decided victory, though the rebels were killed and taken in large numbers. They were of Longstreet's crack division, and had charged with wild yells, confident of victory, but Hayes's men drove them back with tremendous slaughter. The battle had begun an hour before sunset with the attempt of the Union forces to hold a piece of turnpike road, by which a body of cavalry, sent to cut off the supplies in the rear of Early's army, were to rejoin our Kanawha division. Hayes posted his men behind a terrace wall for quarter of a mile along the road, remaining himself on horseback in full sight, while the enemy charged. The enemy came within a few yards. Hayes's men rose with a yell, and struck them with a deadly fire, every shot of which told, and then charged in their turn. The rebels, thrown into wild disorder, turned and ran, pursued to their reserve line, where they rallied and repulsed their pursuers, who took cover in a piece of woods. Now ensued a strange conflict. The commanders on either side were desirous to withdraw their men. Crook sent Hayes word to let the fire die if he could (and the rebels for their part were willing), but not to stop till the enemy stopped. So the men were ordered to let the fire drop, and they fired more and more infrequently, till it came to only a shot at a time; then suddenly three or four would fire by chance together, and on this the whole of both sides would engage again. At last, without the retirement of either army, the surgeons and burying parties from both sides began to mingle together with lanterns, looking for the wounded and the dead between the hosts. Only at the apparition of these spectral lights, flitting hither and thither over the bloody field, and hovering where death or anguish lay, did the battle cease.

Speaking of the engagement afterwards, and especially of the moment when he sat his horse exposed to the full fire of the enemy, while his men lay crouched behind the terrace wall by the roadside, Hayes recognized the peril in which he had been. " But," he added, " I enjoyed the excitement more than ever, — *my men behaved so well !* "

CHAPTER IX.

OPEQUAN, FISHER'S HILL, AND CEDAR CREEK.

THE battle of Opequan was fought on the 19th of September, in the neighborhood of Winchester, where two months before Hayes had so gallantly sustained his first and only defeat. Mr. Reid's vivid and stirring account of the battle gives the highest honor to Hayes, who had the extreme right of Crook's command in making a flank attack. "The position was reached under cover of an almost impenetrable growth of cedar, crossing a swampy stream. Here the division was halted and formed. First brigade (Hayes's) in front, and second (Johnson's) in rear. Throwing out a light line of skirmishers, the brigade advanced rapidly to the front, driving the enemy's cavalry. The national cavalry at the same time advanced out of the woods on the right. After advancing in this way across two or three open fields under a scattering fire, the crest of a slight elevation was reached, when the enemy's infantry line came into view off diagonally to the left front, and he opened a brisk artillery fire. Moving forward double-quick under this fire, the brigade reached a thick fringe of underbrush, dashing through which it came upon a deep slough forty or fifty yards wide, and nearly

waist-deep, with soft mud at the bottom, overgrown
with a thick bed of moss nearly strong enough to bear
the weight of a man. It seemed impossible to get
through it, and the whole line was staggered for a moment. Just then Colonel Hayes plunged in with his
horse, and under a shower of bullets and shells, with his
horse sometimes down, he rode, waded, and dragged his
way through, and after a pause long enough to partially
re-form the line, charged forward again, yelling and
driving the enemy. Sheridan's old cavalry kept close
up on the right, having passed around the slough, and
every time the enemy was driven from cover charged
and captured a large number of prisoners. This plan
was followed throughout the battle, by which the cavalry
was rendered very effective. In one of these charges,
Colonel Duvall, the division commander, was wounded
and carried from the field, leaving Colonel Hayes in
command. He was everywhere, exposing himself reck-
lessly, as usual. He was the first over the slough, he
was in advance of the line half the time afterwards.
Men were dropping all around him, but he rode through
it all as if he had a charmed life.

"No reënforcements, no demonstration as promised;
something must be done to stop the murderous, concen-
trated fire that is cutting the force so dreadfully. Selecting some Saxony rifles in the twenty-third, pieces
of seventy-one calibre, with a range of twelve hundred
yards, Lieutenant McBride was ordered forward with
them to kill the enemy's artillery horses in plain sight.
They moved forward under cover as much as possible.

At the first shot a horse drops; almost immediately another is killed; a panic seems to seize the artillery, and they commence limbering up. The infantry take the alarm, and a few begin running from the intrench-ments. The whole line rises, and with a tremendous yell our men rush frantically from the breastwork, and thus, without stopping to fire another shot, the enemy ran in utter confusion — that terrible cavalry which had been hovering like a cloud on the flanks, sweeping down on the rebels and capturing them by regiments."

Another account of the battle states that the fight began at daylight, and that at noon the tide was rather against the Union forces. It was at this moment, while the rebels in Winchester were rejoicing over the vic-tory, that Hayes's brigade led the charge through the slough. It was in fact a deep creek, with high banks, very boggy margins, and some twenty-five yards in width. The rebel fire burst out in all its fury as the line reached this formidable obstacle. The men wa-vered, but it was death to stop now. Hayes was the first to take the plunge, and his horse was mired under him midway of the slough. He dismounted, and throw-ing himself forward on his hands and knees managed, while the shot and shell struck all round him in the morass, by crawling, swimming, and floundering on, to reach the other shore alone. When he reached the shore, the bank was so steep that the enemy's fire could not strike him, and when he had regained his feet, he turned about to see who was coming next. Captain Ben-jamin F. Stearns, of the thirty-sixth Ohio, a very brave

and gallant officer, was coming next. He was just at
hand as Hayes turned, and his presence undoubtedly
brought great comfort to his commander, there within
twenty-five feet of the rebel line. Hayes raised his
cap, Stearns lifted his, and smiling, the comrades shook
hands. Then Hayes beckoned to his men with his
cap; at once the morass was full of them, swarming
over as they could; and when some two score had
landed, they charged up the bank upon the enemy,
who, never dreaming of an attack at this point, had
left his artillery unsupported. The batteries were
taken, and the whole of Crook's command having
crossed, his men charged a strongly posted rebel line
five hundred yards beyond the first. Their charge was
made in the teeth of a destructive fire; at times they
wavered under the storm of grape and musketry, but
the flags were pushed on, and the straggling crowd
followed. The affair began to look dark, when, " at
the most critical moment," writes Hayes, in a letter
dated two days after the battle, " that splendid cavalry,
with sabres drawn, moved slowly around our right,
beyond the creek, then at a trot, and finally, with
shouts and a gallop, charged right into the rebel lines.
We pushed on, and away broke the rebels."

The battle of Fisher's Hill occurred the day after
that of Opequan. It was, in fact, rather a victory than
a fight, and consisted simply of a wholesale capture of
artillery by our forces, without the loss of a man. The
enemy had retreated some twenty-five miles up the
valley of the Shenandoah to a point where the valley,

narrowing to a breadth of three miles, is traversed by the mountain ridge called Fisher's Hill; and here they had fortified a naturally strong position, and were apparently impregnably intrenched. After consultation between Crook and Sheridan, it was, upon Crook's insistance, resolved not to attack them in front, though it was believed that an army demoralized by so recent defeat could be broken even in that position, but to turn their left. Crook took Hayes's division (by the wounding of Duvall, Hayes was in command of both brigades), and the general and colonel rode together at the head of the men. As the steeper ascent began, all the officers dismounted except Hayes, but he had replaced the charger mired in the slough at Opequan with a teamster's horse, whose surefootedness enabled him to carry his rider anywhere. The force clambered up and down mountain sides and through ravines till they struck the gorge in which the rebels were posted, when Hayes led the charge by galloping right down upon the rebel lines. The whole division followed with a yell, and the rebels — men of Jackson's old corps and Early's veterans — broke and ran in hopeless panic, losing every gun.

Early on the 19th of October the famous battle of Cedar Creek began with the disastrous defeat of our troops under General Wright, who commanded in Sheridan's absence, and suffered himself to be surprised by Early and Longstreet. Anxious for his right flank, he found himself suddenly struck on the left, under cover of a heavy fog, in which his assailants had all the advantages.   In fifteen minutes the enemy was in his camps, and his force thrown into utter confusion and in flight towards Winchester.   A few miles from that place the first fugitives met a major-general on a black horse gayly trotting down the road, who at sight of them quickened his trot to a gallop.   He swung his cap, smiled cheerily, and said, " Face the other way, boys.   We are going back to our camps ; " and as he met regiment after regiment, " Boys, this never would have happened if I had been here.   And now we are going back to our camps."   It was Sheridan, and the rout became a march to victory.   The beaten army turned, drove the enemy from their camp, and broke him to atoms along the whole line, capturing nearly all his transportation, and retaking their lost artillery.   This is the story in brief, but it cannot be too fully told, nor too often.   Mr. Reid's accounts of it in his sketch of Sheridan's life, and his narrative of the twenty-third regiment, are, like all the battle-pieces of his " Ohio in the War," graphic and dramatic, and at the same time admirably clear.   " The situation," he says, " in a few minutes after the attack, was about . this : Crook's command, overpowered and driven from their advanced position, were forming on the left of the nineteenth corps, which corps was just getting into action, the left being hotly engaged, but not so much so as Crook's command yet.   The right of the line had not been engaged at all, and was not for some time after.   While the line was in this situation, the trains were all slowly moving off.   A desperate stand was

made by the shattered lines of Crook's command to
save the head-quarters' train of the army, which came
last from the right, and it succeeded. . . . . From
this time the whole line fell slowly back, fighting stubbornly, to a new position which had been selected.
There they halted, and the enemy seemed content with
shelling us.

"General Crook lay a couple of rods away from the
line, in a place which seemed more particularly exposed
than any other part of the line. Colonel Hayes lay close
by, badly bruised from his fall, and grumbling because
the troops did not charge the enemy's line instead of
waiting to be charged. Suddenly there is a dash in the
rear, on the Winchester pike; and almost before they
are aware, a young man in full major-general's uniform,
and riding furiously a magnificent black horse, literally
'flecked with foam,' reins up and springs off by General Crook's side. There is a perfect roar as everybody
recognizes — SHERIDAN! He talks with Crook a little
while, cutting away at the tops of the weeds with his
riding-whip. General Crook speaks half a dozen sen-
tences that sound a good deal like the crack of the
whip; and by that time some of the staff are up. They
are sent flying in different directions. Sheridan and
Crook lie down and seem to be talking, and all is quiet
again, except the vicious shells of the different batteries,
and the roar of artillery along the line. After a while
Colonel Forsyth comes down in front, and shouts to the
general: "The nineteenth corps is closed up, sir!"
Sheridan jumps up, gives one more cut with his whip,

whirls himself round once, jumps on his horse, and
starts up the line.   Just as he starts off he says to the
men, 'We are going to have a good thing on them
now, boys!' and so he rode off."

In this battle Hayes commanded the Kanawha division, and being in reserve a mile back from the main line,
did not share in its disaster when the rebels attacked.
In the stand made by his division to save the head-quarters, the fighting was very severe, though the men were
disheartened by the belief that the enemy were in the
rear, and were held to their work with difficulty.   At a
certain moment of the fight Hayes saw his right breaking, and rode rapidly down to rally his men, but they
melted away from around him, and left him exposed
alone to the fire of the enemy, who filled the air with a
hail of lead.   He was galloping forward at full speed,
when his horse, struck with a score of balls, was killed
under him; as the horse dropped, the rider was flung
over his head and terribly bruised from crown to heel,
while the ankle of his left foot, catching in the stirrup,
was dislocated.   He lay conscious, but perfectly still,
well knowing that the slightest movement would bring
him a shower of bullets; then at length, watching his
chance, he leaped to his feet and regained his own lines,
after a sharp chase, and mounted his orderly's horse.
He kept his men in some order and shook off the enemy, till the fog lifted, when they began to fight with
more confidence, continually pressed by the enemy, but
retreating slowly and in good order.   After retiring
three or four miles, Hayes joined his force with another

body and succeeded in checking the enemy's advance; his men took rails from the fences and made fires for coffee, and he lay down on the creek bank with Crook and other officers, and talked of the shame of defeat by forces they had beaten so often. Crook wished to attack them, but Wright being in command, nothing was done. At this juncture Sheridan came up, and after a brief parley with Crook, said, " Boys, we will have a good thing, for we will be in our camp before night. Set your watches," and he fixed the minute when they were to move out. At three o'clock they attacked the enemy and surprised him in turn, and the victory followed. In spite of his dislocated ankle and the injuries received in his fall, Hayes was able to keep the saddle throughout the day ; before the close he received another wound, but it was slight; he was struck in the head by a spent ball.

That night, Sheridan, denouncing the manner in which his army had been used by having so many divisions commanded by colonels, said to Hayes, " You will be a brigadier-general from this time." When the promotion actually came, he wrote home a letter so like himself, in due sense of the honor and in decent self-respect, that we shall need no excuse, with the reader at least, in giving it here in full.

" General Crook gave me a very agreeable present this afternoon — a pair of his old brigadier-general straps. The stars are somewhat dimmed with hard service, but will correspond pretty well with my rusty old blouse. Of course, I am very much gratified with the promotion. I know perfectly well that the rank has been conferred on all sorts of small people, and so cheapened shamefully, but I can't help feeling that getting it at the close of a most bloody campaign, on the recommendation of fighting generals like Crook and Sheridan, is a different thing from the same rank conferred — well, as it has been in some instances."

Whilst he was doing all that hard fighting in the valley of the Shenandoah, he had been elected to Congress from the second Ohio district, and he got the news after the battle of Cedar Creek. In one of his admirable letters home he expresses his gratification, but adds : " My *particular* gratification is much less than it would be if I were not so much more gratified by my good luck in winning 'golden opinions' in the more stirring scenes around me here. My share of *notoriety* here is nothing at all, and my *real* share of merit is also small enough, I know ; but the consciousness that I am doing my part in these brilliant actions, is far more gratifying than anything the election brings me."

Between the beginning of May and end of October, 1864, Hayes was under fire on sixty days, and he was under fire on seven hundred days in the course of the war. He was four times wounded, the severest wound being that received at South Mountain. Yet the wound from which he has suffered most is hardly to be called a wound at all. A fragment of shell struck so close to his knee as to cut his pantaloons clean away at that point ; he rode through the day, and never made anything of the affair, but now, after twelve years, this merely approximate hurt troubles him more than all the rest, especially in going up stairs.

It is believed, however, that it will not prevent his ascent of the Capitol steps, on the 4th of March next.

7

ERRATUM.

On page 96, eighth line from bottom, for "seven hundred days," read "about one hundred days."

CHAPTER X

HAYES was first nominated for Congress by the Republicans of the second Cincinnati district in August,
and elected in October, 1864, in the very hottest of
the Shenandoah Valley fighting, when nearly every day
brought its battle, and every day was full of suffering
and danger. The letter which he wrote when the
news of his nomination reached him, with a hint that
his presence in Cincinnati would secure his election, is
as magnanimous as Clay's "I would rather be right
than be President," and its words are such as deserve
to live long after this political campaign, whatever its
results may be, is forgotten. He confesses that though
he had cared very little about being a candidate, he pre-
fers now to succeed after having consented to the use
of his name, but as to the matter of going home on furlough, he adds: "*An officer fit for duty, who at this
crisis would abandon his post to electioneer for Congress,
ought to be scalped. You may feel perfectly sure I shall
do no such thing.*"

He had not, of course, sought the nomination, but at
the urgence of his friends he had let the matter take

its course, and he was elected by a majority which showed that no other Republican could have carried the district. But he did not take his seat in Congress till after the war was over, and the faithful troops he had so long commanded no longer had a foe to face.

After the Shenandoah Valley campaign, his command went into winter quarters and was not engaged afterwards. In the comparative quiet of this time he felt free to ask leave of absence, and he went to Washington to see Lincoln inaugurated, on the 4th of March, 1865 (having first paid a brief visit to his family in Ohio), and then returned to camp. The news of the President's murder came to him with shocking force after so recently witnessing his entry upon a second term of beneficent power, and Hayes immediately wrote to his wife a letter too good in itself, and too significant in many ways, to be omitted from this record. It is not merely a testimony to character and feeling on his part, but it is suggestive of her enlightened sympathy with him in matters of public concern, and hints of qualities of mind and heart in her more common to the White House in the days of Mrs. Washington and of Mrs. Madison than in our own.

"NEW CREEK, WEST VIRGINIA, 16*th April* (Sunday), 1865.

"When I heard first, yesterday morning, of the awful tragedy at Washington, I was pained and shocked to a degree I have never before experienced. I got on to the cars, then just starting, and rode down to Cumberland. The probable consequences, or rather the possible results, in their worst imaginable form, were pre-

sented to my mind, one after the other, until I really
began to feel that here was a calamity so extensive
that in no direction could be found any, the slightest
glimmer, of consolation. The nation's great joy turned
suddenly to a still greater sorrow ! A ruler tested and
proved in every way, and in every way found equal to
the occasion, to be exchanged for a new man whose
ill-omened beginning made the nation hang its head !
Lincoln for Johnson ! The work of reconstruction,
requiring so much statesmanship, just begun ! The
calamity to Mr. Lincoln in a personal point of view
so uncalled for a fate ! — so undeserved, so unpro-
voked ! The probable effect upon the future of public men in this country, the necessity for guards ; our
ways to be assimilated to those of the despotisms of
the old world — and so I would find my mind filled
only with images of evil and calamity, until I felt a
sinking of heart hardly equaled by that which oppressed us all when the defeat of our army at Manassas,
almost crushed the nation. But slowly, as in all cases
of great affliction, one comes to feel that it is not all
darkness ; the catastrophe is so much less, happening
now, than it would have been at any time before, since
Mr. Lincoln's election. At the period after his first
inauguration ; at any of the periods of great public
confusion ; during the pendency of the last presidential election ; at any time before the defeat of Lee,
such a calamity might have sealed the nation's doom.
Now, the march of events can't be stayed, probably
can't be much changed. It is possible that a greater

degree of severity in dealing with the rebellion may be ordered, and *that* may be for the best. As to Mr. Lincoln's name and fame and memory, — all is safe. His firmness, moderation, goodness of heart; his quaint humor, his perfect honesty and directness of purpose, his logic, his modesty, his sound judgment and great wisdom; the contrast between his obscure beginnings and the greatness of his subsequent position and achievements; his tragic death, giving him almost the crown of martyrdom, elevate him to a place in history second to none other in ancient or modern times. His success in his great office, his hold upon the confidence and affections of his countrymen, we shall all *say* are only second to Washington's; we shall probably *feel* and *think* that they are not *second* even to his."

In April, Hayes, to his own regret and the grief of his old brigade, was transferred to a new command under Hancock,[1] and he was the leader of that expedi-

---

[1] Hayes bade his old command farewell in terms expressive of the strong affection existing between them : —

"It is with very great regret that I have been compelled to part with the officers and men of the first brigade. With many of you I have been associated in the service almost four years; with three of the regiments of the brigade more than two years, and with all the regiments during the memorable campaign of 1864. The battle of Cloyd Mountain; the burning of New River bridge, and the night march over Salt Pond Mountain under General Crook in May; the days and nights of marching, fighting, and starving on the Lynchburg raid in June; the defeat at Winchester, and the retreat on the 24th and 25th of July; the skirmishing, marching, and countermarching in the Shenandoah Valley in August; the bloody and brilliant victories in September; the night battle at Berryville ; the turn-

tion against Lynchburg which was given up after Lee's surrender and the ruin of the Confederacy. Shortly after, the work being done and other work calling him, he sent in his resignation, which took effect on the 1st of June. But before he left the army he had the glory of participating in the grand review at Washington; and no one in all those hundred thousands had a better right to the triumph of that great day than this honest man, this faithful soldier, this stainless patriot.

ing of the enemy's left at Sheridan's battle of Winchester; the avalanche which swept down North Mountain upon the rebel stronghold at Fisher's Hill; the final conflict in October; the surprise and defeat of the morning, and the victory of the evening at Cedar Creek, — these and a thousand other events and scenes in the campaign of 1864 form part of our common recollections which we are not likely ever to forget. As long as they are remembered, we shall be reminded of each other and of the friendly and agreeable relation which so long existed between us.

"It is very gratifying to me that I was allowed to serve with you until we received together the tidings of the great victory which ends the rebellion. Whatever may be your fortune, I shall not cease to feel a lively interest in everything which concerns your welfare and reputation."

Hayes himself afterwards came to acquiesce in the change, but his old brigade was not so easily consoled. One of his officers wrote: —

"WINCHESTER, VIRGINIA, *April* 20, 1865.

"When I learned that you were taken away from us, I was so in-dignant I could hardly refrain from language considered highly un-military; not that I have aught against our present brigade commander — for he has my confidence and respect — but because I think that by a just and equitable title, sealed with blood, dearly bought, and fairly won, *this is your brigade*. In this war men become attached to each other by more than common ties. I have been clear 'through the mill;' from Washington to Chattanooga; you are my choice of all the brigade commanders I have been under, save and except Crook."

In October, Hayes returned to Cincinnati and re-opened his old house, and in December he took his seat in Congress, where he at once made himself quietly felt as a thorough and diligent worker. Two or three ingrained habits of his life forbade him to make him-self conspicuous on the floor. In the first place, as we have already repeatedly shown, it was Hayes's cus-tom to study any new business and fit himself for suc-cess in it, and congressmanship was an entirely new business to him. Then he is a man whose inherent modesty and self-respect are at one in keeping him aloof from any mere noisy exhibition of himself, or from attempting anything which he believes the greater ex-perience of others will enable them to perform better. Above all, his army life had given him an ever-increas-ing contempt of unnecessary and intrusive eloquence, and he wrote to a friend, — one of many eager that he should distinguish himself in the usual congressional way, — "I am disgusted at the shameful waste of time and patience the so-called orators of Washington make," and he refused to "distinguish himself" accordingly. He went to work as chairman of the library com-mittee, and urged the extension and increase of the library. Chiefly by his efforts, the space and material were increased threefold; the Force Historical Library was added to that of Congress, and the Smithsonian Library transferred to it. He was instrumental in the purchase of many valuable works, and on the com-mittee, his artistic taste as well as his literary knowl-edge were felt. No vote of his ever favored the purchase of trashy pictures or sculptures, and he constantly advocated the selection of known and able artists for government commissions.

On other committees he was a conscientious worker, knowing that the real business of legislation is done across the committee tables, and not by the speechifyers on the floor of the House.

His first vote was given for a resolution requiring the maintenance of the public faith " sacred and inviolable " from " any attempt to scale or repudiate " the national debt; and he early introduced and carried through a resolution to provide for the special punishment of agents or attorneys defrauding soldiers and sailors in the matter of their pensions and bounties. Renominated by acclamation in 1866, and reëlected by a majority which showed a gain while the rest of the ticket showed a loss, he continued especially to interest himself in behalf of the soldiers, and as a commander singularly beloved and trusted by his men he was, of course, overwhelmed with their claims and applications.

He refused here, as always, to make his office a means of office ; he did his duty, and let his future take care of itself. He was always in his seat ; he never shirked responsibility or dodged a vote ; he voted with his party on all the measures of reconstruction, and he was incessantly active in a personal as well as public way in securing the passage and ratification of the thirteenth and fourteenth amendments.

Even before taking his seat in Congress, he was

meditating retirement from public life, either to his uncle's farm in Fremont, or his own law practice in Cincinnati, and nothing but the sense of public duty prevailed with him to accept the nomination for governor of Ohio, offered him in 1869. He gave up his place in Congress, however, to meet an emergency of national significance, and in a campaign conducted with all the fire of a nature kindled through and through by his experiences in fighting the same ideas on the battle-field, he beat his opponent, the present Senator Thurman, by a majority that no one else could have commanded. The questions at issue were the reconstruction measures, which the Democrats assailed, taking their stand upon a platform prepared by the late Mr. Vallandigham, (whose course, only more open than that of Mr. Tilden in the war it is merciful not to remember,) and practically in favor of State supremacy. The canvass was very excited, and Hayes and Thurman spoke daily throughout the State, alternately attacking each other's positions, and replying and rejoining almost for the hundredth time. Hayes's personal popularity gave the Republicans their governor, but the legislature and the constitutional amendment was lost by fifty thousand majority. That legislature, therefore, refused to ratify the amendments, and it elected Mr. Thurman to the United States Senate.

In 1869 Hayes was renominated in the Republican convention by acclamation; and the Democrats nominated General Rosecrans. That gallant soldier refused to stand on a platform declaring that the whole bonded

debt should be paid in greenbacks, and embodying whatever existed of enmity to the cause for which he had
fought, and the nomination was passed on to Mr. Pendleton, who hesitatingly accepted, and was duly beaten
at the October elections.

It has been well known in Ohio that Hayes could
have been easily elected United States Senator in the
place of Mr. Sherman in 1872, if he had been the man
to profit by prosperous chances at the expense of a
friend whom he honored and admired. The Republican
majority in the legislature was small, and enough of
the Republicans were disaffected to form with the willing Democrats (always personally fond of Hayes) the
number requisite to choose him. But he promptly
and severely discouraged the movement, and the man
who ought to have been elected, and who was the choice
of the greater part of the Republicans, succeeded where
a sordid or selfish rival could have secured his defeat.

At the end of his second term as governor, Hayes
wished to retire from political life. " I, too," he wrote
to a friend, " mean to be out of politics. The ratification of the fifteenth amendment" (this had in the mean
time taken place) "gives me the boon of equality before the law, terminates my enlistment, and discharges
me cured."   His letters and journal entries are to the
same effect.   His interest in public affairs was still intense, but personally he did not care any longer to take
part in them. "In spite of his protests," as the dispatch announcing the fact ran, he was nominated in his
old Cincinnati district in 1872 by the Republicans, who

had not ceased to ask for the use of his name, and who had used it against his express desire. He went down and made the canvass, delivering some of his best speeches, but the reaction against Republicanism had set in so strongly that he was beaten, though by a majority not half so great as that which defeated his fellow Republican in the other Cincinnati district. He declined the appointment of Assistant United States Treasurer at Cincinnati, offered him by Grant, and retired to Fremont. His uncle Birchard, his life-long benefactor and friend, died in 1874, leaving him a handsome fortune, and Hayes made the good old man's house his home, planning to live there a life of leisure and of books, not unmindful of good citizenship, but no longer troubled by the cares and responsibilities of active politics.

His journals of this period form a curious study of such a man in the fulfillment of such a purpose. His keen delight in nature is oddly mingled with his inextinguishable interest in public affairs. He sets down in the same entry the aspects of the weather and the probable effects of such and such measures upon the party and the country. He records the fact that he has put away his sleigh for the season, but we find that he has not put away his uneasiness about the currency. A robin who steals a whole spool of thread for his nest, and hopelessly entangling himself, hangs dangling by the neck in one of the dooryard trees, does not affect him more than the spectacle of the Democratic politicians who promise themselves prosperity on an excess of greenbacks. Nevertheless the domestic and agricultural interests do finally prevail, and there are long spaces in the diaries where politics are never mentioned — where the thermometer completely displaces the President.

In 1875 Ohio had had for one term a Democratic governor for the first time in nearly twenty years — a very good governor, as far as economical administration went, and a very bad governor, as far as ideas on the currency went: William Allen, namely, of untainted personal character, but politically besotted with seventy years of unmitigated Democracy. He was strong with his party, he was strong with the people, and how to get rid of a man so much worse than any worse man was a vital question with the Republicans.

Hayes had been approached in his philosophical retirement at Fremont, but though flattered with the prospect of being a third time governor, as an honor never before conferred on any citizen of Ohio, he had thought the matter over, and he decidedly refused to let his name go before the convention. It became day by day more apparent that the Republicans could succeed with no other name, and that without it the cause of honest money and of public self-respect must be lost. Still Hayes refused, and upon the knowledge of his determined refusal, his old friend, Judge Taft, of Cincinnati, afterwards Secretary of War, allowed himself to be proposed in the convention. The convention nominated Hayes, and then made his nomination unanimous. A dispatch was sent to Hayes, who, considering the circumstances under which his friend had suffered himself to appear as a candidate for nomination, felt doubly bound to decline. He stood reading over the form of his refusal with a friend, when a second dispatch arrived, saying that Judge Taft's name had been withdrawn by Mr. Taft, his son, and that it was upon Mr. Taft's motion that Hayes's nomination had been made unanimous. Hayes tore up his refusal and accepted; and now ensued the famous campaign of 1875, which made Ohio the national battle-ground, where Hayes, Schurz, Sherman, Woodford, Morton, Dawes, Oglesby, Garfield, Taft, and Windom supported the cause of good sense and good faith in currency against the inflationists, who are now the friends of that eminent and disinterested hard-money man, Mr. Tilden.

Another very important element in the canvass, especially urged by Hayes, was the question of secular against ecclesiastical education. The Democratic party, always prompt to make use of whatever is reactionary in our civilization, had already in its brief term of power in Ohio made haste to truckle to the priest-led foreigners, who demanded a division of the school-fund. Hayes insisted upon the political recognition of the fact known to us all, that our system of free secular schools, with all its errors and short-comings, was the very basis of our liberties, and that any division of the school-fund meant chaos come again. He thoroughly aroused people and politicians to a sense of this; the liberal Germans and the freedom-loving voters of all the churches made common cause against the priests, and the triumph that ensued was owing, far more than has been realized, to the abhorrence excited by the attempt upon the public schools. If any reader here fancies himself beguiled with a travesty of Italian story, let him turn to the Catholic journals of Ohio, and see how bold was the assault, and how real the danger. Of Catholics as religionists, Hayes is no enemy, but he is the relentless enemy of Catholics as Catholic politicians, just as he would be the enemy of Methodists as Methodist politicians.

Hayes has now been some five years governor of Ohio, and though often thwarted by Democratic legislation, has succeeded in reducing the State debt $2,773,406, and the State tax from 3.5 mills on the dollar to 2.9, with an annual saving of $914,593. By continued pressure upon the legislature he reduced the local taxation throughout the State more than $17,000,000, and through his influence local authorities were forbidden by law to make any large expenditure without the sanction of a popular vote — wherein the people of Ohio are much freer than those of Massachusetts. He also secured the passage of a law prohibiting municipalities from incurring debts beyond the amounts actually in their treasuries. These measures he has urged in the prime of a life whose dearest action was spent in the tented field, and was never for a moment sullied by association with ring-thieves. His principle of retrenchment is not a mere twelvemonth old, nor his patriotism the growth of the years since the nation was made. He helped to make it, and his public economies are the expression of a life-long private honesty.

So, also, his devotion to civil service reform is not merely a profitable novelty. Eight years ago he supported Jenckes's bill, and six years ago he recommended in one of his messages the amendment of the Ohio constitution, so as to make civil service reform a part of the organic law. He did more ; he showed his faith by his works. When he became governor, he was importuned by old and dear friends, to turn out the Democratic State librarian, and give the office, one of the few in the governor's gift, to a most worthy and competent Republican. He refused.

"The present incumbent" (he wrote) "of the librarianship is a faithful, painstaking old gentleman with a family of invalid girls dependent on him. His courtesy and evident anxiety to accommodate all who visit the library have secured him the indorsement of almost all who are in the habit of using the books, and under the circumstances I cannot remove him. Old associations, your fitness, and claims draw me the other way, but you see, etc., etc. Very sincerely,   R. B. HAYES."

Of course the pressure brought to bear upon a governor in such a case is as nothing compared to the pressure brought to bear upon the President, but it is the same in kind though so different in quantity, and it would be very interesting indeed to know whether Mr. Tilden can point to a single Republican whom he has kept in office because he was "painstaking, faithful, and courteous."

Among other reforms, Hayes has repeatedly urged upon the legislature the adoption of some form of minority representation, and the passage of registration laws to secure the purity of elections, and he has never ceased to urge. the punishment of malfeasance in office. The highest testimony to the purity of his administration is to be found on the lips of his enemies — his political enemies; he has only friends, personally. At the end of his second term, the Democrats appointed a committee to investigate the administration of affairs under him. This was the chairman's report: —

" The special committee appointed under House resolution No. 113 report as follows: The examination has taken a wide range. One hundred and nine witnesses, residing in various parts of the State, have been subpœnaed and examined touching public contracts and expenditures, construction of public buildings, conduct of public institutions, etc. All matters, without reference to the date of their occurrence, coming to the knowledge of the committee, that seemed to promise any probability of throwing any light upon the subjects of inquiry, or any of them, have been diligently inquired into.

" Your committee take pleasure in reporting that, so far as elective officers and their subordinates are concerned, very commendable honesty and fidelity have been observed, and that in the official conduct of no public officer, whether elective or appointive, has corruption been disclosed."

As governor, Hayes has been tireless in the promotion of schemes of public beneficence and advantage, such as the removal of the incurably insane from the jails and poorhouses to fitting quarters in the State asylums, the establishment of a reform school for girls and a reform farm for boys, greater humanity as well as greater economy in the management of the State prison, and above all the founding of a soldiers' and sailors' orphans' home. His heart, never insensible to the claim of friendless sorrow, quick to the misery alike of the incurable insane and of the curable depraved, was most deeply touched by the condition of the children of those who died for freedom and nationality. " During the war for the Union," he wrote in his second annual message, " the people of this State acknowledged their obligation to support the families of their absent soldiers, and undertook to meet it, not as a charity, but as a partial compensation justly due for services rendered. The nation is saved, and the obligations to care for the orphans of the men who died to save it still remain to be fulfilled. It is officially estimated that three hundred soldiers' orphans, during the past year, have been inmates of the county infirmaries of the State. It is the uniform testimony of the directors of county infirmaries that those institutions are wholly unfit for children ; that in a majority of cases they are sadly neglected, and that even in the best infirmaries the children are subject to the worst moral influences. Left by the death of their patriotic fathers in this deplorable condition, it is the duty of the State to assume their guardianship, and to provide support, education, and homes to all who need them."

8

Again, in his second inaugural he said: "Under the providence of God the people of this State have greatly prospered. But in their prosperity they cannot forget 'him who hath borne the battle, nor his widow nor his orphan,' or the thousands of other sufferers in our midst who are entitled to sympathy and relief. They are to be found in our hospitals, our infirmaries, our asylums, our prisons, and in the abodes of the unfortunate and the erring. The Founder of our religion, whose spirit should pervade our laws, and animate those who enact and those who enforce them, by his teaching and his example has admonished us to deal with all the victims of adversity as the children of our common Father."

It is not alone in the gentle and sober feeling of passages like this that Hayes reminds us of Lincoln; much also in the essential modesty, the quiet firmness, the unaggressive self-respect of our leader recalls the man who had a genius for being simply great.

A very important public work recommended and urged to completion by Hayes is the geological survey of Ohio, which has not only been of great use to science, but of incalculable material advantage to Ohio, in the development of her mineral resources. In fine, every project for the enlightened advancement of the public interest, morals, or taste, during the years since Hayes has been governor, has had him for its author or its powerful and effective friend.[1]

1 For a full account of Hayes's gubernatorial services and administrations, we refer the reader to the conscientious and painstaking chapters in Mr. J. Q. Howard's Life of Hayes. (Robert Clarke & Co., Cincinnati.)

But we can no longer dwell upon this period of his history, for we now approach the moment when from being a man of national importance he became also a man of national note.   He had not been elected governor in 1875 before he began to be President in Ohio. As soon as his election was known, a newspaper of the old Giddings and Garfield district, representing the perennial political right-mindedness of the " Western Reserve," printed his name as candidate, and throughout the whole vast State the prophetic instinct of his supreme fitness began to possess the people, though at first the Republican and the conditionally Republican press were by no means united upon him.   '

As for himself, he seems to have given himself no concern about the presidency, but to have gone quietly about his business of governor.   No man could hear himself much talked of for the chief place in a nation like this without feeling some share of the popular excitement, but no man was less capable of pushing himself for such a place than Hayes.   We have seen many letters of his, written during the period when the movement in his favor was gathering strength and form (a fact which every Ohioan felt in his bones, however insensible the osseous structure of Eastern Republicans remained), and they all point to the fact that, while he was not indifferent to it, he was firmly resolved to have nothing to do with it.

In one of these letters, shown us by his correspondent, he wrote : " I am not pushing, directly or indirectly.   It is not likely that I shall.   If the sky falls we shall all catch larks. On the topics you name, a busy seeker after truth would find my views in speeches and messages, but I shall not help him to find them. I appreciate your motives and your friendship. But it is not the thing for you or me to enroll ourselves in the great army of office-seekers. Let the currents alone."

This was the tenor of all his expressions. From his diary we permit ourselves a single paragraph, which not only shows his mind in March last, but also shows the man as he has been all his life: tranquilly self-reliant, high-purposed, and resolute never to act from personal ambition. " With so general an impression in my favor in Ohio, and a fair degree of assent elsewhere, especially in States largely settled by Ohio people, I have supposed that it was possible I might be nominated. But with no opportunity and no desire to make combinations or to lay wires, I have not thought my chances worth much consideration. I feel less diffidence in thinking of this subject than perhaps I ought. It seems to me that good purposes, and the judgment, experience and firmness I possess would enable me to execute the duties of the office well. I do not feel the least fear that I should fail ! "

After the Ohio State convention met and instructed its delegates to vote for Hayes in the national convention, his attitude changed only so far as was involved in a feeling of allegiance to his friends, and a sense of his obligation not to embarrass their efforts in his behalf. This is not the time, and this is not the place to say whom Hayes expected to be nominated at Cincinnati, but we know upon the authority of those constantly about him at the time that he did not at all expect the nomination for himself until the sixth ballot, and then when the result came on the seventh ballot he could scarcely accept the fact as true.

We need not weary the reader with the twice-told tale of the convention's proceedings, but we cannot deny ourselves the pleasure of reproducing entire in this place the exquisitely fitting speech in which ex-Governor Noyes of Ohio presented Hayes's name.

GENTLEMEN: On behalf of the forty-four delegates from Ohio, representing the entire Republican party of Ohio, I have the honor to present to this convention the name of a gentleman well known and favorably known throughout the country; one held in high respect, and much beloved by the people of Ohio; a man who, during the dark and stormy days of the rebellion, when those who are invincible in peace and invisible in battle were uttering brave words to cheer their neighbors on, himself, in the fore-front of battle, followed his leaders and his flag until the authority of our government was established from the Lakes to the Gulf, and from the river round to the sea; a man who has the rare good fortune since the war was over to be twice elected to Congress from the district where he resided, and subsequently the rarer fortune of beating successively for the highest office in the gift of the people of Ohio, Allen G. Thurman, George H. Pendleton,

and William Allen. He is a gentleman who has somehow fallen into the habit of defeating Democratic aspi-
rants for the presidency, and we in Ohio all have a
notion that from long experience he will be able to do
it again. In presenting the name of Governor Hayes,
permit me to say we wage no war upon the distinguished gentlemen whose names have been mentioned
here to-day. They have rendered great service to
their country, which entitles them to our respect and
to our gratitude. I have no word to utter against
them. I only wish to say that General Hayes is the
peer of these gentlemen in integrity, in character, in
ability. They appear as equals in all the great qualities which fit men for the highest positions which the
American people can give them. Governor Hayes is
honest; he is brave; he is unpretending; he is wise,
sagacious, a scholar, and a gentleman. Enjoying an
independent fortune, the simplicity of his private life,
his modesty of bearing, is a standing rebuke to the extravagance — the reckless extravagance — which leads
to corruption in public and in private places.

Remember now, delegates to the convention, that
a responsible duty rests upon you. You can be governed by no wild impulse. You can run no fearful
risks in this campaign. You must, if you would succeed, nominate a candidate here who will not only carry
the old, strong Republican States, but who will carry
Indiana, Ohio, and New York, as well as other doubtful States. We care not who the man shall be, other
than our own candidate. Whoever you nominate, men

of the convention, shall receive our heartiest and most earnest efforts for their success. But we beg to submit that in Governor Hayes you have those qualities which are calculated best to compromise all difficulties, and to soften all antagonisms. He has no personal enemies. His private life is so pure that no man has ever dared assail it. His public acts throughout all these years have been above suspicion, even. I ask you then if, in the lack of these antagonisms and with all of these good qualities, living in a State which holds its election in October, the result of which will be decisive, it may be, of the presidential campaign, it is not worth while to see to it that a candidate is nominated against whom nothing can be said, and who is sure to succeed in the campaign?

In conclusion, permit me to say that, if the wisdom of this convention shall decide at last that Governor Hayes's nomination is safest and is best, that decision will meet with such responsive enthusiasm here in Ohio as will insure Republican success at home, and which will be so far-reaching and wide-spreading as to make success almost certain from the Atlantic to the Pacific.

With his name thus presented, and with the forty-four Ohio delegates faithfully, ballot after ballot, throwing in his favor the weight of what was best in the sentiment of a State so eminent in war, so wise in the uses of peace, his final success was, in the opinion of those skilled in judging such matters, only a question of time.

This history is by no means too dignified to tell how the news came to the lady who, we hope, is soon to renew the best traditions of the White House. She was absent from home on a visit of mercy at one of the State asylums, and a carriage was sent to recall her. The driver was charged with no message except that she was to return home at once, and she drove back in alarmed expectation of some domestic calamity, merely to find that her husband had been nominated for the presidency.

CHAPTER XI.

THE sum of all these positions and opinions is the now famous letter of acceptance, which the whole party joyfully ratified and made its political creed. It shall be given in full, and then we shall show how it is merely the final expression of principles and ideas long since expressed by its author.

THE LETTER OF ACCEPTANCE.

COLUMBUS, OHIO, *July* 8, 1876.

Hon. Edward McPherson, Hon. Wm. A. Howard, Hon. Joseph H. Rainey, and others, Committee of the Republican National Convention.

GENTLEMEN, — In reply to your official communication of June 17th, by which I am informed of my nomination for the office of President of the United States by the Republican National Convention at Cincinnati, I accept the nomination with gratitude, hoping that under Providence I shall be able, if elected, to execute the duties of the high office as a trust for the benefit of all the people.

I do not deem it necessary to enter upon any extended examination of the declaration of principles

made by the convention.   The resolutions are in accord
with my views, and I heartily concur in the principles
they announce.   In several of the resolutions, however,
questions are considered which are of such importance
that I deem it proper to briefly express my convictions
in regard to them.

The fifth resolution adopted by the convention is of
paramount interest.   More than forty years ago, a system of making appointments to office grew up, based
upon the maxim, " To the victors belong the spoils."
The old rule — the true rule — that honesty, capacity,
and fidelity constitute the only real qualifications for
office, and that there is no other claim, gave place to
the idea that party services were to be chiefly considered.
All parties, in practice, have adopted this system.   It
has been essentially modified since its first introduction.
It has not, however, been improved.

At first, the President, either directly or through the
heads of departments, made all the appointments.   But
gradually the appointing power, in many cases, passed
into the control of members of Congress.   The offices,
in these cases, have become not merely rewards for
party services, but rewards for services to party leaders.
This system destroys the independence of the separate
departments of the government; it tends directly to extravagance and official incapacity ; it is a temptation to
dishonesty ; it hinders and impairs that careful super-
vision and strict accountability by which alone faithful
and efficient public service can be secured; it obstructs
the prompt removal and sure punishment of the un-

worthy. In every way it degrades the civil service and the character of the government. It is felt, I am confident, by a large majority of the members of Congress, to be an intolerable burden, and an unwarrantable hindrance to the proper discharge of their legitimate duties. It ought to be abolished. The reform should be thorough, radical, and complete.

We should return to the principles and practice of the founders of the government, supplying by legislation, when needed, that which was formerly established custom. They neither expected nor desired from the public officer any partisan service. They meant that public officers should owe their whole service to the government and to the people. They meant that the officer should be secure in his tenure as long as his personal character remained untarnished and the performance of his duties satisfactory. If elected, I shall conduct the administration of the government upon these principles; and all constitutional powers vested in the executive will be employed to establish this reform.

The declaration of principles by the Cincinnati convention makes no announcement in favor of a single presidential term. I do not assume to add to that declaration; but, believing that the restoration of the civil service to the system established by Washington and followed by the early presidents can be best accomplished by an executive who is under no temptation to use the patronage of his office to promote his own re-election, I desire to perform what I regard as a duty, in stating now my inflexible purpose, if elected, not to be a candidate for election to a second term.

On the currency question I have frequently expressed my views in public, and I stand by my record on this subject. I regard all the laws of the United States relating to the payment of the public indebtedness, the legal tender notes included, as constituting a pledge and moral obligation of the government, which must in good faith be kept. It is my conviction that the feeling of unce ainty inseparable from an irredeemable paper currency, with its fluctuations of values, is one of the great obstacles to a revival of confidence and business, and to a return of prosperity. That uncertainty can be ended in but one way — the resumption of specie payments; but the longer the instability connected with our present money system is permitted to continue, the greater will be the injury inflicted upon our economical interests and all classes of society.

If elected, I shall approve every appropriate measure to accomplish the desired end, and shall oppose any step backward.

The resolution with respect to the public school system is one which should receive the hearty support of the American people. Agitation upon this subject is to be apprehended, until, by constitutional amendment, the schools are placed beyond all danger of sectarian control or interference. The Republican party is pledged to secure such an amendment.

The resolution of the convention on the subject of the permanent pacification of the country, and the complete protection of all its citizens in the free enjoyment of all their constitutional rights, is timely and of great importance. The condition of the Southern States attracts the attention and commands the sympathy of the people of the whole Union. In their progressive recovery from the effects of the war, their first necessity is an in'elligent and honest administration of government, which will protect all classes of citizens in all their political and private rights. What the South most needs is peace, and peace depends upon the supremacy of law. There can be no enduring peace if the constitutional rights of any portion of the people are habitually disregarded. A division of political parties resting merely upon distinctions of race, or upon sectional lines, is always unfortunate, and may be disastrous. The welfare of the South, alike with that of every other part of the country, depends upon the attractions it can offer to labor, to immigration, and to capital. But laborers will not go, and capital will not be ventured, where the constitution and the laws are set at defiance, and distraction, apprehension, and alarm take the place of peace-loving and law-abiding social life. All parts of the constitution are sacred, and must be sacredly observed, the parts that are new no less than the parts that are old. The moral and material prosperity of the Southern States can be most effectively advanced by a hearty and generous recognition of the rights of all by all, a recognition without reserve or exception.

With such a recognition fully accorded, it will be practicable to promote, by the influence of all legitimate agencies of the general government, the efforts of the people of those States to obtain for themselves the blessings of honest and capable local government.

If elected, I shall consider it not only my duty, but it will be my ardent desire, to labor for the attainment of this end.

Let me assure my countrymen of the Southern States that if I shall be charged with the duty of organizing an administration, it will be one which will regard and cherish their truest interests — the interests of the white and of the colored people both, and equally; and which will put forth its best efforts in behalf of a civil policy which will wipe out forever the distinction between North and South in our common country.

With a civil service organized upon a system which will secure purity, experience, efficiency, and economy; with a strict regard for the public welfare, solely, in appointments; with the speedy, thorough, and unsparing prosecution and punishment of all public officers who betray official trusts; with a sound currency; with education unsectarian and free to all; with simplicity and frugality in public and private affairs, and with a fraternal spirit of harmony pervading the people of all sections and classes, we may reasonably hope that the second century of our existence as a nation will, by the blessing of God, be preëminent as an era of good feeling, and a period of progress, prosperity, and happiness.

Very respectfully,   Your fellow-citizen,

R. B. HAYES.

CIVIL SERVICE REFORM.

In this letter the first and most important matter touched is that of the civil service, in which, as we have already seen, Hayes had long before been a practical reformer. He had also constantly urged the reform in private and in public, officially and personally. Jenckes's and Trumbull's bills had received his vote and hearty approval, and to a friend he had written early in March, 1870, " I agree with you perfectly in the spoils doctrine. This you would know if you had read my last inaugural. I am glad you do not bore yourself with such reading generally, but you are in for it now, and I shall send you a copy." " For many years," he said, addressing a legislature of that Democratic party which invented the present infamous system, " political influence and political services have been essential qualifications for employment in the civil service, whether State or national. As a general rule, such employments are regarded as terminating with the defeat of the political party under which they began. All political parties have adopted this rule. In many offices the highest qualifications are only obtained by experience. Such are the positions of the warden of the penitentiary and his subordinates, and the superintendents of asylums and reformatories and their assistants. But the rule is applied to these as well as to other offices and employments. A change in the political character of the executive and legislative branches of the government is followed by a change of the officers and employees in all of the departments and institutions of the State. Efficiency and fidelity to duty do not prolong the employment; unfitness and neglect of duty do not always shorten it. The evils of this system in State affairs are, perhaps, of small moment compared with those which prevail under the same system in the transaction of the business of the national government. But at no distant day they are likely to become serious, even in the administration of State affairs. The number of persons employed in the various offices and institutions of the State must increase, under the most economical management, in equal ratio with the growth of our population and business.

"A radical reform in the civil service of the general government has been proposed. The plan is to make qualifications, and not political services and influence, the chief test in determining appointments, and to give subordinates in the civil service the same permanency of place which is enjoyed by officers of the army and navy. The introduction of this reform will be attended with some difficulties. But in revising our State constitution, if this object is kept constantly in view, there is little reason to doubt that it can be successfully accomplished."

In his annual message of January, 1871, he recurred to the subject of civil service, and urged its reformation through the prompt punishment of frauds. "What the public welfare demands," he said, "is a practical measure which will provide for a thorough and impartial investigation in every case of suspected neglect, abuse, or fraud. Such an investigation, to be effective, must be made by an authority independent, if possible, of all local influences. When abuses are discovered, the prosecution and punishment of offenders ought to follow. But even if prosecutions fail in cases of full exposure, public opinion almost always accomplishes the object desired. A thorough investigation of official corruption and criminality leads with great certainty to the needed reform. Publicity is a great corrector of official abuses. Let it therefore be made the duty of the governor, on satisfactory information that the public good requires an investigation of the affairs of any public office or the conduct of any public officer, whether State or local, to appoint one or more citizens who shall have ample powers to make such investigation. If by the investigation violations of law are discovered, the governor should be authorized, in his discretion, to notify the attorney-general, whose duty it should be, on such notice, to prosecute the offenders. The constitution makes it the duty of the governor to ' see that the laws are faithfully executed.' Some such measure as the one here recommended is necessary to give force and effect to this constitutional provision."

Again, in a speech which he made in 1872, he advocated a complete reform in almost the exact terms of the letter of acceptance.

"There are," he declared, "several questions relating to the present and the future which merit the attention of the people. Among the most interesting of these is the question of civil service reform.

9

" About forty years ago a system of making appointments to office grew up, based on the maxim, ' To the victors belong the spoils.' The old rule — the true rule — that honesty, capacity, and fidelity constitute the highest claim to office, gave place to the idea that partisan services were to be chiefly considered. All parties in practice have adopted this system. Since its first introduction it has been materially modified. At first the President, either directly or through the heads of departments, made all appointments. Gradually, by usage, the appointing power in many cases was transferred to members of Congress — to senators and representatives. The offices in these cases have become not so much rewards for party services as rewards for personal services in nominating and electing senators and representatives. What patronage the President and his cabinet retain, and what offices congressmen are by usage entitled to fill is not definitely settled. A congressman who maintains good relations with the executive usually receives a larger share of patronage than one who is independent. The system is a bad one. It destroys the independence of the separate departments of the government, and it degrades the civil service. It ought to be abolished. General Grant has again and again explicitly recommended reform. A majority of Congress has been unable to agree upon any important measure. Doubtless the bills which have been introduced contain objectionable features. But the work should be begun. Let the best obtainable bill be passed, and experience will show what amendments are required. I would support either Senator Trumbull's bill or Mr. Jenckes's bill, if nothing better were proposed. The admirable speeches on this subject by the representative of the first district, the Hon. Aaron F. Perry, contain the best exposition I have seen of sound doctrine on this question, and I trust the day is not distant when the principles which he advocates will be embodied in practical measures of legislation. We ought to have a reform of the system of appointments to the civil service, thorough, radical, and complete."

It is not necessary to expatiate on these positions, so distinct and so explicit that there is no mistaking them. Taken in connection with the expressions of the letter of acceptance, and the facts of Hayes's gubernatorial administrations, they show that civil service reform has been his settled conviction and his practice for the last eight years. He was one of the very first friends of the reform, and it is simply absurd to compare with him on this ground a man who was the political ally of public plunderers when Hayes was urging administrational purity and efficiency by precept and example.

CURRENCY.

In regard to honest money, — the duty of the government to keep its promises to pay to the last mill, — Hayes now stands where he has stood ever since his political thinking began, ever since his boyhood. For the last year, his success has been the expression of the people's will in this direction ; he is, in fact, the most

eminent exemplification of the public sense of honor
on this point. No other man represents as he does at
this moment the popular idea that just debts should be
fully paid, and in nowise shirked or evaded. His
speeches and letters and private diaries so abound with
opinions to this effect, that it is hard to choose from
them. ·

In a speech delivered at Glendale in 1872, from
which we have already given some passages on civil
service reform, he handled the no less vital question
with as frank a touch. "We want a financial policy so
honest that there can be no stain on the national honor
and no taint on the national credit; so stable that
labor and capital and legitimate business of every sort
can confidently count upon what it will be the next
week, the next month, and the next year. We want
the burdens of taxation so justly distributed that they
will bear equally upon all classes of citizens in propor-
tion to their ability to sustain them. We want our
currency gradually to appreciate until, without financial
shock or any sudden shrinkage of values, but in the
natural course of trade, it shall reach the uniform and
permanent value of gold. With lasting peace assured,
and a sound financial condition established, the United
States and all of her citizens may reasonably expect to
enjoy a measure of prosperity without a parallel in the
world's history."

He was not only always right in this matter, but he
always felt sure of the people's good sense and honesty,
and he entered upon the famous campaign of 1875 in

the full confidence that " if the party in power were opposed to a sound, safe, stable currency . . . . the people would make a change." He conducted the canvass upon the principle that there was a sense of justice and of self-respect in the popular heart which would finally respond to his own, and while his opponents appealed to the people's self-interest and all the sordid motives that prompt human nature, he steadily addressed their reason and their consciences.

A few passages from one of the many speeches he made on the currency question will serve to show the simple, direct, quiet fashion in which he dealt with hearers whom he assumed to be equally willing with himself to think and to do right. The speech in question was made at Marion, Ohio, on the 31st of last July. "The most important part," he said, " in fact the only important part of the Democratic platform in Ohio this year, which receives or deserves much attention, is that in which is proclaimed a radical departure on the subject of money from the teachings of all of the Democratic fathers. This Ohio Democratic doctrine inculcates the abandonment of gold and silver as a standard of value. Hereafter gold and silver are to be used. as money only ' where respect for the obligation of contracts requires payment in coin.' The only currency for the people is to be paper money, issued directly by the general government, 'its volume to be made and kept equal to the wants of trade,' and with no provision whatever for its redemption in coin. The Democratic candidate for lieutenant-governor, who

opened the canvass for his party, states the money issue
substantially as I have.   General Cary, in his Barnes-
ville speech, says : —

" ' Gold and silver, when used as money, are redeem-
able in any property there is for sale in the nation,
will pay taxes for any debt, public or private.   This
alone gives them their money value.   If you had a
hundred gold eagles, and you could not exchange them
for the necessaries of life, they would be trash, and you
would be glad to exchange them for greenbacks or anything else that you could use to purchase what you
require.   With an absolute paper money, stamped by
the government and made a legal tender for all purposes, its functions as money are as perfect as gold or
silver can be ! '

" This is the financial scheme which the Democratic
party asks the people of Ohio to approve at the election in October.   The Republicans accept the issue.
Whether considered as a permanent policy or as an ex-
pedient to mitigate present evils, we are opposed to it.
It is without warrant in the constitution, and it violates
all sound financial principles.

" The objections to an inflated and irredeemable
paper currency are so many that I do not attempt to
state them all.   They are so obvious and so familiar
that I need not elaborately present or argue them.   All
of the mischief which commonly follows inflated and
inconvertible paper money may be expected from this
plan, and in addition it has very dangerous tendencies,
which are peculiarly its own.   An irredeemable and in-

flated paper currency promotes speculation and extravagance, and at the same time discourages legitimate business, honest labor, and economy. It dries up the true sources of individual and public prosperity. Over-trading and fast living always go with it. It stimulates the desire to incur debt; it causes high rates of interest; it increases importations from abroad; it has no fixed value; it is liable to frequent and great fluctuations, thereby rendering every pecuniary engagement precarious, and disturbing all existing contracts and expectations. It is the parent of panics. Every period of inflation is followed by a loss of confidence, a shrinkage of values, depression of business, panics, lack of employment, and widespread disaster and distress. The heaviest part of the calamity falls on those least able to bear it. The wholesale dealer, the middle-man, and the retailer always endeavor to cover the risks of the fickle standard of value by raising their prices. But the men of small means and the laborer are thrown out of employment, and want and suffering are liable soon to follow.

"When government enters upon the experiment of issuing irredeemable paper money, there can be no fixed limit to its volume. The amount will depend on the interest of leading politicians, on their whims, and on the excitement of the hour. It affords such facility for contracting debt that extravagant and corrupt government expenditure are the sure result. Under the name of public improvements the wildest enterprises, contrived for private gain, are undertaken. Indefinite expansion becomes the rule, and in the end bankruptcy, ruin, and repudiation.

" During the last few years a great deal has been said about the centralizing tendency of recent events in our history. The increasing power of the government at Washington has been a favorite theme for Democratic declamation. But where, since the foundation of the government, has a proposition been seriously entertained which would confer such monstrous and dangerous powers on the general government as this inflation scheme of the Ohio Democracy? During the war for the Union, solely on the ground of necessity, the government issued the legal-tender or greenback currency. But they accompanied it with a solemn pledge, in the following words of the act of June 30, 1864 : —

" ' Nor shall the total amount of United States notes issued or to be issued ever exceed four hundred millions, and such additional sum, not exceeding fifty millions, as may be temporarily required for redemption of temporary loans.'

" But the Ohio inflationists, in a time of peace, on grounds of mere expediency, propose an inconvertible paper currency, with its volume limited only by the discretion or caprice of its issuers, or their judgment as to the wants of trade. The most distinguished gentleman whose name is associated with the subject once said, ' The process must be conducted with skill and caution, ... by men whose position will enable them to guard against any evil,' and using a favorite illustration he said, ' The secretary of the treasury ought to be able to judge. His hand is upon the pulse of the country. He can feel all the throbbings of the blood in the arteries. He can tell when the blood flows too fast and strong, and when the expansion should cease.' This brings us face to face with the fundamental error of this dangerous policy. The trouble is, the pulse of the patient will not so often decide the question as the interest of the doctor. No man, no government, no Congress is wise enough and pure enough to be trusted with this tremendous power over the business and property and labor of the country. That which concerns so intimately all. business should be decided, if possible, on business principles, and not be left to depend on the exigencies of politics, the interests of party, or the ambition of public men. It will not do for property, for business, or for labor to be at the mercy of a few political leaders at Washington, either in or out of Congress. The best way to prevent it is to apply to paper money the old test sanctioned by the experience of all nations — let it be convertible into coin. If it can respond to this test, it will, as nearly as possible, be sound, safe, and stable. . . . .

" The credit of the nation depends on its ability and disposition to keep its promises. If it fails to keep them, and suffers them to depreciate, its credit is tainted, and it must pay high rates of interest on all of its loans. For many years we must be a borrower in the markets of the world. The interest-bearing debt is over seventeen hundred millions of dollars. If we could borrow money at the same rate with some of the great nations of Europe, we could save perhaps two per cent. per annum on this sum. Thirty or forty millions a year we are paying on account of tainted credit. The more promises to pay an individual issues, without redeeming them, the worse becomes his credit. It is the same with nations. The legal-tender note for five dollars is the promise of the United States to pay that sum in the money of the world, in coin. No time is fixed for its payment. It is therefore payable on presentation — on demand. It is not paid; it is past due; and it is depreciated to the extent of twelve per cent. The country recognizes the necessities of the situation, and waits, and is willing to wait, until the productive business of the country enables the government to redeem. But the Columbus financiers are not satisfied. They demand the issue of more promises. This is inflation. No man can doubt the result. The credit of the nation will inevitably suffer. There will be further depreciation. A depreciation of ten per cent. diminishes the value of the present paper currency from fifty to one hundred millions of dollars. Its effect on business would be disastrous in the extreme. The present legal tenders have a certain steadiness, because there is a limit fixed to their amount. Public opinion confides in that limit. But let that limit be broken down, and all is uncertainty. The authors of this scheme believe inflation is a good thing. When this subject was under discussion, a few years ago, the 'Cincinnati Enquirer' said, 'The issue of two millions dollars of currency would only put it in the power of each voter to secure $400 for himself and family to spend in the course of a life-time. Is there any voter thinks that is too much — more than he will want?' This shows what the platform means. It means inflation without limit; and inflation is the downward path to repudiation. It means ruin to the nation's credit, and to all individual credit. All the rest of the world have the same standard of value. Our promises are worthless as currency the moment you pass our boundary line. Even in this country, very extensive sections still use the money of the world. Texas, the most promising and flourishing State of the South, uses coin. California and the other Pacific States and Territories do the same. Look at their condition. Texas and California are not the least prosperous part of the United States. This scheme cannot be adopted. The opinion of the civilized world is against it. The vast majority of the ablest newspapers of the country is against it. The best minds of the Democratic party are against it. The last three Democratic candidates for the presidency were against it. The German citizens of the United States, so distinguished for industry, for thrift, and for soundness of judgment in all practical money affairs, are a unit against it. The Republican party is against it. The people of Ohio will, I am confident, decide in October to have nothing to do with it."

After all, however, in this matter of honest money, as in all others, the nearer you can come to Hayes, the more of a man you find him, and a letter of his, not

written for the public eye, shows better than any med-
itated utterance how sturdily steadfast he continues in
the principles of common sense and of common justice.

EXECUTIVE DEPARTMENT, STATE OF OHIO, COLUMBUS, }
March 4, 1876. }

MY DEAR GENERAL GARFIELD, — I have your
note of 2d. I am kept busy with callers, correspond-
ence, and the routine details of the office, and have
not therefore tried to keep abreast of the currents of
opinion on any of the issues. My notion is that the
true contest is to be between inflation and a sound currency. The Democrats are again drifting all to the
wrong side. We need not divide on details, on methods, or time when.

The previous question will again be irredeemable
paper as a permanent policy, or a policy which seeks a
return to coin. My opinion is decidedly against yielding a hair's breadth.

We can't be on the inflation side of the question.
We must keep our face, our front, firmly in the other
direction. "*No steps backward*," *must be something more* ·
than unmeaning platform words. "The drift of sentiment among our friends in Ohio," which you inquire
about, will depend on the conduct of our leading men. It
is for them to see that the right sentiment is steadily
upheld. We are in a condition such that firmness and
adherence to principle are of peculiar value just now.
I would "consent" to no backward steps. To yield or
compromise is weakness, and will destroy us. If a
better resumption can be substituted for the present

one, that may do. But keep cool. *We can better afford to be beaten in Congress than to back out.*

Sincerely, R. B. HAYES.

RECONSTRUCTION AND PACIFICATION.

On all the measures of reconstruction, Hayes, while
in Congress, constantly voted with the Republican
party, and his judgment and heart were alike in their
favor. Outside of Congress he was active in securing
the adoption of the constitutional amendments; as governor, "believing that the measure was right, and that
the people approved of it," he recommended the ratification of the fifteenth amendment; and he duly had the
pleasure of certifying to the general government the
fact of its adoption. He held that "the United
States were not a confederacy bound together by a
mere treaty or compact, but a nation," in which equality
was "an equality of rights." It was his firm belief
that "the first and highest duty of the people of the
North to themselves, to the South, to their country,
and to God, was to crush the rebellion," and that "after
the suppression of the rebellion, the next plain duty of
the national government was to see that the lives, liberty, and property of all classes of citizens were secure,
and especially to see that the loyal white and colored
citizens who resided, or might sojourn in those States,
did not suffer injustice, oppression, or outrage because
of their loyalty."

In a speech made during his campaign against Thurman in 1867, he dealt with fallacies which are as impu-
dently proposed to-day as they were then : —

" Our adversaries are accustomed to talk of the rebellion as an affair which began when the rebels attacked Fort Sumter in 1861, and which ended when
Lee surrendered to Grant in 1865.   It is true that the
attempt by force of arms to destroy the United States
began and ended during the administration of Mr. Lincoln.   But the causes, the principles, and the motives
which produced the rebellion are of an older date than
the generation which suffered from the fruit they bore,
and their influence and power are likely to last long after
that generation passes away.   Ever since armed rebellion failed, a large party in the South have struggled
to make participation in the rebellion honorable, and
loyalty to the Union dishonorable.   The lost cause
with them is the honored cause.   In society, in business, and in politics, devotion to treason is the test of
merit, the passport to preferment.   They wish to return
to the old state of things, *an oligarchy of race and the
sovereignty of States.*

" To defeat this purpose, to secure the rights of man,
and to perpetuate the national Union, are the objects
of the congressional plan of reconstruction.   That plan
has the hearty support of the great generals (so far as
their opinions are known) — of Grant, of Thomas, of
Sheridan, of Howard — who led the armies of the
Union which conquered the rebellion.   The statesmen
most trusted by Mr. Lincoln and by the loyal people of
the country during the war also support it.   The
supreme court of the United States, upon formal application and after solemn argument, refuse to interfere

with its execution. The loyal press of the country, which did so much in the time of need to uphold the patriot cause, without exception are in favor of the plan."

In the same effort — so nobly free from the arts of the rhetorician and the clap-trap of the politician — he said of the proposal to enfranchise the blacks : —

" There are now within the limits of the United States about five millions of colored people. They are not aliens or strangers. They are here not by the choice of themselves or of their ancestors. They are here by the misfortune of their fathers and the crime of ours. Their labor, privations, and sufferings, unpaid and unrequited, have cleared and redeemed one third of the inhabited territory of the Union. Their toil has added to the resources and wealth of the nation untold millions. Whether we prefer it or not, they are our countrymen, and will remain so forever.

" They are more than countrymen — they are citizens. Free colored people were citizens of the colonies. The constitution of the United States, formed by our fathers, created no disabilities on account of color. By the acts of our fathers and of ourselves, they bear equally the burdens, and are required to discharge the highest duties of citizens. They are compelled to pay taxes and to bear arms. They fought side by side with their white countrymen in the great struggle for independence, and in the recent war for the Union. In the revolutionary contest colored men bore an honorable part, from the Boston Massacre, in 1770, to the surrender of Cornwallis, in 1781. Bancroft says : ' Their

names may be read on the pension rolls of the country
side by side with those of other soldiers of the Revolution.' In the war of 1812, General Jackson issued an
order complimenting the colored men of his army engaged in the defense of New Orleans. I need not
speak of their number or of the war of the rebellion.
The nation enrolled and accepted them among her de-
fendants to the number of about two hundred thousand,
and in the new regular army act, passed at the close of
the rebellion by the votes of Democrats and Union
men alike, in the Senate and in the House, and by the
assent of the President, regiments of colored men,
cavalry and infantry, form part of the standing army
of the republic.

" In the navy, colored American sailors have fought
side by side with white men from the days of Paul
Jones to the victory of the Kearsarge over the rebel
pirate Alabama. Colored men will, in the future as in
the past, in all times of national peril, be our fellow-
soldiers. Tax-payers, countrymen, fellow-citizens, and
fellow soldiers, the colored men of America have been
and will be. It is now too late for the adversaries of
nationality and human rights to undertake to deprive
these tax-payers, freemen, citizens, and soldiers of the
right to vote.

" Slaves were never voters. It was bad enough that
our fathers, for the sake of union, were compelled to
allow masters to reckon three fifths of their slaves for
representation, without adding slave suffrage to the
other privileges of the slave-holder. But free colored

men were always voters in many of the colonies, and in several of the States, North and South, after independence was achieved. They voted for members of the Congress which declared independence, and for members of every Congress prior to the adoption of the federal constitution; for the members of the convention which framed the constitution; for the members of many of the State conventions which ratified it, and for every President from Washington to Lincoln.

"Our government has been called the white man's government. Not so. It is not the government of any class, or sect, or nationality, or race. It is a government founded on the consent of the governed, and Mr. Broomall, of Pennsylvania, therefore properly calls it 'the government of the governed.' It is not the government of the native born, or of the foreign born, of the rich man, or of the poor man, of the white man, or of the colored man — it is the government of the freeman. And when colored men were made citizens, soldiers, and freemen, by our consent and votes, we were estopped from denying to them the right of suffrage."

Up to the present moment Hayes has receded from none of his positions upon reconstruction, and as to the pacification of the South he has never ceased to desire and promote it. But as the French philosopher said in assenting to the proposition that capital punishment should be abolished: "Very well; let the murderers begin." No white man throughout the whole length and breadth of the South, no matter how rebellious he may have been; no ex-Confederate steeped in Northern blood, will be molested by President Hayes in the rights of his restored citizenship; no Southerner who does not fear justice need fear him. And this fact Southerners understand as well as we. It is the banded murderers who slay in secret and openly, who violate the rights of other men to life, liberty, and the pursuit of happiness — it is these alone who have cause to dread his election, not such true men as the writer of the following letter, who differs from tens of thousands of others in the South only in publicly avowing what they privately feel to be true.

GALVESTON, *April* 18, 1876.

HON. A. B. NORTON:

DEAR SIR, — I am indebted to your kindly feeling for the intelligence of the 18th inst., containing your article on Governor R. B. Hayes and "old Kenyon," the *alma mater* of each of us.

I have seen with much pleasure and satisfaction that Governor Hayes has been frequently mentioned by the press, and unanimously nominated by the Republican convention of Ohio, for the presidency of the United States.

Although I am, and have long been from principle, a Democrat, and expect to support and vote the Democratic ticket at the next presidential election, yet I hope Governor Hayes will receive the nomination of the Republican party; for, if your party should be successful, there is no distinguished member of it I would rather see President than Rutherford B. Hayes, for I know him well, and I believe that he is honest, that he is capable, and that he will be faithful to the constitution. Having been in Congress four years, and governor of Ohio the third time, he has experience, and is a statesman of incorruptible integrity, besides being a genial and dignified gentleman, a scholar, a sound lawyer and patriot — one who, if elected, would be President for the whole country, and not for a section. What the South most needs is *good local government*, and one in the presidential chair who will do all he can under the constitutions, Federal and State, to promote it. I believe, if elected, Hayes will do this.

In addition to what I have said, I will add that he has, of my own knowledge, a personal interest in our State. He spent the winter and part of the spring of 1848 and 1849 in Texas. Since then he has kept up his interest in our State, and to-day has a better Texan library than many of our own educated citizens. In the first speech of his late political campaign (which he sent me), he spoke of Texas in the most complimentary manner. I can most truthfully say that my old classmate, and almost life-long friend, Rutherford B. Hayes, deserves all and more than all that you have said of him; and I believe, if he should be chosen President, that he will make such a President as to secure the confidence of the South as well as the North; and if any one of your party can bring back the Monroe era of good feeling in politics, it is R. B. Hayes.

Very truly, etc.,   GUY M. BRYAN.

The reader will remember the writer of this letter, and will honor his frankness and loyalty to his old friend in a section where the terror of social ostracism, quite as much as political conviction, will reduce the white vote for Hayes to a minimum. Southerners like him have the sympathy and compassion of all right-thinking Northern men, and they may rest secure in Mr. Bryan's confidence. But neither they nor any one could make a greater mistake than to suppose that Hayes is one of the vulgar sentimentalists who would barter the sacred and terrible memories of the past for a moment óf unmeaning effusion ; one of the witless and heartless milksops who befoul, in their brutal phrase of the "bloody shirt," the fame of those who died on battle-field and in prison-pen during the war, and have since perished in the same cause by assassination all over the South.

SECULAR FREE EDUCATION.

On this point, as on all others, Hayes has had perfect confidence in the people. At a serenade given him in Columbus after his last nomination for governor, he said : "If it shall turn out that the party in power is dangerously allied to any body of men who are opposed to our free schools, and have proclaimed undying hostility to our educational system, then I doubt not the people will make a change in the administration." And in his speech at Marion in the same canvass he treated the question at length. "Altogether the most interesting questions in our State affairs," he said, "are

those which relate to the passage, by the last legislature, of the Geghan bill [to provide Catholic books for
prisoners in the pententiary], and the war which the
sectarian wing of the Democratic party is now waging
against the public schools. In the admirable speech
made by Judge Taft at the Republican State convention, he sounded the key-note to the canvass on this
subject. He said, 'Our motto must be universal liberty
and universal suffrage, secured by universal education.'
Before we discuss these questions, it may be well, in
order that there may be no excuse for further misrep-
resentation, to show by whom this subject was introduced into politics, and to state explicitly that we attack no sect and no man, either Protestant or Jew,
Catholic or unbeliever, on account of his conscientious
convictions in regard to religion. Who began the agitation of this subject? Why is it agitated? All parties
have taken hold of it. The Democratic party in their
State convention make it the topic of their longest resolution. In their platform they gave it more space
than any other subject except the currency. Many
of the Democratic county conventions also took action
upon it.

"The Republican State convention passed resolutions on the question. It is stated that it was considered in about forty Republican county conventions.
The State Teachers' Association, at their last meeting,
passed unanimously the following resolution. Mr. Tap-
pan, from the committee on resolutions, reported the
following : —

"'*Resolved,* That we are in favor of a free, impartial, and unsectarian education for every child in the State, and that any division of the school fund or appropriation of any part thereof to any religious or private school would be injurious to education and the best interests of the church.'

"The assemblies of the different religious denominations in the State which have recently been held have generally, and I think without exception, passed similar resolutions. If blame is to attach to all who consider and discuss this question before the public, we have had a very large body of offenders. But I have not named all who are engaged in it. I have not named those who began it; those who for years have kept it up; those who in the press, on the platform, in the pulpit, in legislative bodies, in city councils, and in school boards, now unceasingly agitate the question. Everybody knows who they are; everybody knows that the sectarian wing of the Democratic party began this agitation, and that it is bent on the destruction of our free schools. . . . .

"The sectarian agitation against the public schools was begun many years ago. During the last few years it has steadily and rapidly increased, and has been encouraged by various indications of possible success. It extends to all of the States where schools at the common expense have been long established. Its triumphs are mainly in the large towns and cities. It has already divided the schools, and in a considerable degree impaired and limited their usefulness. The glory of the

American system of education has been that it was so
cheap that the humblest citizen could afford to give his
children its advantages, and so good that the man of
wealth could nowhere provide for his children anything
better. This gave the system its most conspicuous
merit. It made it a republican system. The young
of all conditions of life are brought together and educated on terms of perfect equality. The tendency of
this is to assimilate and to fuse together the various
elements of our population, to promote unity, harmony,
and general good-will in our American society. But
the enemies of the American system have begun the
work of destroying it. They have forced away from
the public schools, in many towns and cities, one third
or one fourth of their pupils, and sent them to schools
which it is safe to say are no whit superior to those
they have left. These youth are thus deprived of the
associations and the education in practical republicanism and American sentiments which they peculiarly
need. Nobody questions their constitutional and legal
right to do this, and to do it by denouncing the public
schools. Sectarians have a lawful right to say that
these schools are 'a relict of paganism — that they are
godless,' and that 'the secular school system is a social cancer.' But when, having thus succeeded in dividing the schools, they make that a ground for abol-
ishing school taxation, dividing the school fund, or
otherwise destroying the system, it is time that its
friends should rise up in its defense.

."We all agree that neither the government nor

political parties ought to interfere with religious sects. It is equally true that religious sects ought not to interfere with the government or with political parties. We believe that the cause of good government and the cause of religion both suffer by all such interference. But if sectarians make demands for legislation of political parties, and threaten that party with opposition at the elections in case the required enactments are not passed, and if the political party yields to such threats, then those threats, those demands, and that action of the political party become a legitimate subject of political discussion, and the sectarians who thus interfere with the legislation of the State are alone responsible for the agitation which follows.

" And now a few words as to the action of the last legislature on this subject. After an examination of the Geghan bill, we shall perhaps come to the conclusion that in itself it is not of great importance. I would not undervalue the conscientious scruples on the subject of religion of a convict in the penitentiary, or of any unfortunate person in any State institution. But the provision of the constitution of the State covers the whole ground. It needs no awkwardly framed statute of doubtful meaning, like the Geghan bill, to accomplish the object of the organic law.

" The author of the bill wrote, ' the members claim that such a bill is not needed.' The same opinion prevails in New Jersey, where a similar bill is said to have been defeated by a vote of three to one. But the sectarians of Ohio were resolved on the passage of this bill. Mr. Geghan, its author, wrote to Mr. Murphy, of Cinciunati : —

"'We have a prior claim upon the Democratic party. The elements composing the Democratic party in Ohio to-day are made up of Irish and German Catholics, and they have always been loyal and faithful to the interests of the party. Hence the party is under obligations to us, and we have a perfect right to demand of them, as a party, inasmuch as they are in control of the State legislature and State government, and were by both our means and votes placed where they are to-day, that they should, as a party, redress our grievances.'

"The organ of the friends of the bill published this letter, and among other things said : —

"'The political party with which nine tenths of the Catholic voters affiliate, on account of past services that they will never forget, now controls the State. Withdraw the support which Catholics have given to it, and it will fall in this city, county, and State as speedily as it has risen to its long lost position and power. That party is now on trial. Mr. Geghan's bill will test the sincerity of its professions.'

"That threat was effectual. The bill was passed, and the sectarian organ therefore said : —

"'The unbroken solid vote of the Catholic citizens of the State will be given to the Democracy at the fall election.'

"In regard to those who voted against the bill, it said : 'They have dug their political grave ; it will not be our fault if they do not fill it. When any of them ap-

pear again in the political arena, we will put upon them
a brand that every Catholic citizen will understand.'
No defense of this conduct of the last legislature has
yet been attempted. The facts are beyond dispute.
This is the first example of open and successful sectarian interference with legislation in Ohio. If the
people are wise, they will give it such a rebuke in October that for many years, at least, it will be the last.

" But it is claimed that the schools are in no danger.
Now that public attention is aroused to the importance
of the subject, it is probable that in Ohio they are safe.
But their safety depends on the rebuke which the people shall give to the party which yielded last spring at
Columbus to the threats of their enemies. It is said
that no political party 'desires the destruction of the
schools.' I reply, no political party 'desired' the passage of the Geghan bill; but the power which hates
the schools passed the bill. The sectarian wing of the
Democratic party rules that party to-day in the great
commercial metropolis of the nation. It holds the bal-
ance of power in many of the large cities of the country. Without its votes, the Democratic party would
lose every large city and county in Ohio, and every
Northern State. In the presidential canvass of 1864,
it was claimed that General McClellan was as good a
Union man as Abraham Lincoln, and that he was as
much opposed to the rebellion. An eminent citizen of
this State replied: 'I learn from my adversaries.
Whom do the enemies of the Union want elected?
The man they are for, I am against.' So I would say

to the friends of the public schools: 'How do the enemies of universal education vote?' If the enemies of the free schools give their 'unbroken, solid vote' to the Democratic ticket, the friends of the schools will make no mistake if they vote the Republican ticket."

ONE TERM FOR PRESIDENT.

We find nothing in Hayes's published writings or speeches, before the letter of acceptance, bearing upon this point. But there are other evidences that he was deliberately arriving at it, and we take leave to think that a man who has dwelt so long, so closely, and so penetratingly upon all questions bearing upon administration has probably considered it more thoroughly and wisely than any of his critics.

In regard to reforms not spoken of in the letter of acceptance, the reader will be glad to see that Hayes's progress had been constant and in the right direction. His views upon the chief of these must suffice.

ELECTIVE JUDICIARY A FAILURE.

" Our judicial system is plainly inadequate to the wants of the people of the State. Extensive alterations of existing provisions must be made. The suggestions I desire to present in this connection are as to the manner of selecting judges, their terms of office, and their salaries. It is fortunately true that the judges of our courts have heretofore been, for the most part, lawyers of learning, ability, and integrity. But it must be remembered that the tremendous events and the wonderful progress of the last few years are working great changes in the condition of our society. Hitherto, population has been sparse, property not unequally distributed, and the bad elements which so frequently control large cities have been almost unknown in our State. But with a dense population crowding into towns and cities, with vast wealth accumulating in the hands of a few persons or corporations, it is to be apprehended that the time is coming when judges elected by popular vote, for short official terms, and poorly paid, will not possess the independence required to protect individual rights. Under the national constitution, judges are nominated by the executive and confirmed by the Senate, and hold office during good behavior. It is worthy of consideration whether a return to the system established by the fathers is not the dictate of the highest prudence. I believe that a system under which judges are so appointed, for long terms and with adequate salaries, will afford to the citizen the amplest possible security that impartial justice will be administered by an independent judiciary." (Inaugural of 1870.)

ECONOMICAL STATE AND LOCAL ADMINISTRATIONS.

" One of the most valuable articles of the present State constitution is that which prohibits the State, save in a few exceptional cases, from creating any debt, and which provides for the payment at an early day of the debt already contracted. I am convinced that it would be wise to extend the same policy to the creation

of public debts by county, city, and other local authorities. The rule, ' Pay as you go,' leads to economy in
public as well as in private affairs; while the power to
contract debts opens the door to wastefulness, extravagance, and corruption." (Annual Message, 1871.)

TAXES TO BE VOTED BY TAX-PAYERS.

" The constitution makes it the duty of the legislature to restrict the powers of taxation, borrowing
money, and the like, so as to prevent their abuse. I
respectfully suggest that the present laws conferring
these powers on local authorities require extensive
modification, in order to comply with this constitutional
provision. Two modes of limiting these powers have
the sanction of experience. All large expenditures
should meet the approval of those who are to bear
their burden. Let all extraordinary expenditures
therefore be submitted to a vote of the people, and
no tax be levied unless approved by a majority of all
the voters of the locality to be affected by the tax, at a
special election, the number of voters to be ascertained
by reference to the votes cast at the State election
next preceding such special election. Another mode is
to limit the rate of taxation which may be levied and
the amount of debt which may be incurred. It has
been said that with such restrictions upon the powers
of local authorities, the legislature will be importuned
and its time wasted in hearing applications for special
legislation. The ready answer to all such applications
by local authorities will be to refer them to their own

citizens for a decision of the question. The facility with which affirmative votes can be obtained under the pressure of temporary excitement upon propositions authorizing indebtedness may require further restrictions upon the power to borrow money. It is therefore suggested, for your consideration, to limit the amount of debt for a single purpose, and the total amount for all purposes which any local authority may contract to a certain percentage of the taxable property of such locality." (Annual Message, 1869.)

" The attention of the legislature has often been earnestly invoked to the rapid increase of municipal and other local expenditures, and the consequent augmentation of local taxation and local indebtedness. This increase is found mainly in the cities and large towns. It is certainly a great evil. How to govern cities well, consistently with the principles and methods of popular government, is one of the most important and difficult problems of our time. Profligate expenditure is the fruitful cause of municipal misgovernment. If a means can be found which will keep municipal expenses from largely exceeding the public necessities, its adoption will go far towards securing honesty and efficiency in city affairs. In cities, large debts and bad government go together. Cities which have the lightest taxes and smallest debts are apt, also, to have the purest and most satisfactory governments.

" It is not enough to require in every grant of special authority to incur debt, as a condition precedent, that the people interested shall approve it by their votes.

It is well known how easily such elections are carried under the influence of local excitement and local rivalries. If the rule of the State constitution which forbids all debts except in certain specified emergencies is deemed too stringent to be applied to local affairs, the legislature should at least accompany every authority to contract debt with an imperative requirement that a tax sufficient to pay off the indebtedness within a brief -period shall be immediately levied, and thus compel every citizen who votes to increase debts to vote at the same time for an immediate increase of taxes sufficient to discharge them." (Inaugural, January, 1876.)

PURITY OF THE FRANCHISE.

" The most important subject of legislation which, in my judgment, requires the attention of the General Assembly at its present session, relates to the prevention of frauds upon the elective franchise. Intelligent men of all parties are persuaded that at the recent important State and national elections great abuses of the right of suffrage were practiced. I am not prepared to admit that the reports commonly circulated and believed in regard to such abuses would, so far as the elections in Ohio are concerned, be fully sustained by a thorough investigation of the facts. But it is not doubted that, even at the elections in our own State, frauds were perpetrated to such an extent that all good citizens earnestly desire that effective measures may be adopted by you to prevent their repetition. No elaborate attempt to portray the consequences of this evil is required. If it is allowed to increase, the confidence of the people in the purity of elections will be lost, and the exercise of the right of suffrage will be neglected. To corrupt the ballot-box is to destroy our free institutions. Let all good citizens, therefore, unite in enacting and enforcing laws which will secure honest elections." (Annual Message, November, 1868.)

MINORITY REPRESENTATION.

" All agree that a republican government will fail, unless the purity of elections is preserved. Convinced that great abuses of the elective franchise cannot be prevented under existing legislation, I have heretofore recommended the enactment of a registry law, and also of some appropriate measure to secure to the minority, as far as practicable, a representation upon all boards of elections. There is much opposition to the enactment of a registry law. Without yielding my own settled convictions in favor of such a law, I content myself, in this communication, with urging upon your attention a measure of reform in the manner of conducting elections, the importance and justice of which no one ventures to deny. The conduct of the officers whose duty at elections it is to receive and count the ballots, and to make returns of the result, ought to be above suspicion. This can rarely be the case where they all belong to the same political party. A fair representation of the minority will go far, not only to prevent fraud, but, what is almost of equal importance, to remove the suspicion of fraud. I do not express any preference for any particular plan of securing minority representation in the boards of judges and clerks of elections. Various modes have been suggested, and it will not be difficult to adopt a means of attaining the desired result which will harmonize with our system of election law." (Annual Message, 1869.)

11

CHAPTER XII.

CHARACTER: POLITICIAN, ORATOR, PUBLIC SERVANT,
SOLDIER, CITIZEN, MAN.

WE should have written to little purpose if we had
not already given the reader some distinct idea of the
sort of man of whom we have been treating: a man
who, if you look at him from the side of motive, is as
grandly simple a figure as any of " the simple great
ones gone forever and ever by," but who on his intellectual side has the due modern complexity. One of
the anomalies which most strikes the observer of his
character is the iron *fight* which instantly replaces what
seems the normal repose, almost indifference, of his
nature, when once he is called into action of any sort.
Before battle, when not actually charging the enemy,
he was perfectly tranquil; but when the moment came,
his tranquillity was found heated through, and till the
end arrived his ardor knew no abatement. In his after
political life the same traits appeared, and the man who
never sought an office, who rigidly refused to advance
himself before a convention, had no sooner accepted a
nomination and become responsible for the success of
a principle, than he threw himself into the work with
a fury that at first astonished, and always dismayed his
enemies.

Some life-long habits of his peculiarly fit him for success in a political campaign. He has been, as we have already shown, a constant student of men from his boyhood, and he has been as thorough a political observer for as long a time. Every political event of the smallest significance, every politician of whatever calibre, has a place in his relentless memory; he knows the whole country politically, with only less fullness than he knows Ohio. In addition to this, he has had the habit of compiling history from the newspapers as it was made, and from these collections he has been able at any time to confront an opponent with the record of that opponent's political life from the outset. In certain formidable little books, Mr. Thurman, and Mr. Pendleton, and Mr. Allen successively found that he had full and accurate trace of their political turns and windings; that a man who had nothing to regret in his own past had forgotten nothing in theirs. When these little books were opened on the stump, and their contents supplemented from his unfailing memory, it was like the opening of the books of doom for any hapless politician anxious about his record.

Whoever met Hayes in political conflict knew that his warfare would be unsparing; yet such has always been the personal charm of the man, the quality of his high and blameless character, that the bitterest of his political enemies has been glad to have him for his friend in social life. At the end of a campaign of unwonted fierceness, when, last autumn, his success threw into retirement a man too old to hope for any future triumph, the election of Hayes was confessedly more acceptable to Mr. Allen than that of any other Republican could have been. "If we must have a Republican, I am glad it is Hayes," said the ex-governor to the enterprising interviewer at once set upon him. Let us hope that Mr. Tilden will be able to console himself with equal magnanimity, when his turn comes.

On the stump, Hayes is grave, simple, and earnest. He is no great teller of stories, no maker of laughter; the fine, rather delicate humor of his intimate life rarely appears in arguments pressed solidly home to his listeners' sense of right. We shall give some idea of his method of dealing with an opponent by quoting passages from a speech delivered in the campaign against Thurman, but these can convey but a fragmentary impression after all. If the reader will substitute another name for Thurman's, he can hardly fail to believe that Hayes was prophetically arraigning Mr. Tilden eight years ago. These are the passages from his speech.

"I will quote also from Judge Thurman himself. In a speech lecturing one of his colleagues, who thought the Mexican war was unnecessary, he says: —

" ' It is a strange way to support one's country right or wrong, to declare after war has begun, when it exists both in law and in fact, that the war is aggressive, unholy, unrighteous, and damnable on the part of the government of that country, and on that government rests its responsibility and its wrongfulness. It is a strange way to support one's country right or wrong in

a war, to tax one's imagination to the utmost to depict
the disastrous consequences of the contest; to dwell on
what it has already cost and what it will cost in future ;
to depict her troops prostrated by disease and dying
with pestilence; in a word, to destroy, as far as possible, the moral force of the government in the struggle,
and hold it up to its own people and the world as the
aggressor that merits their condemnation. It was for
this that I arraigned my colleague, and that I intend to
arraign him. It was because his remarks, as far as
they could have any influence, were evidently calculated
to depress the spirits of his own countrymen, to lessen
the moral force of his own government, and to inspire
with confidence and hope the enemies of his country.'

" He goes on further to say : —

" ' What a singular mode it was of supporting her in
a war to bring against the war nearly all the charges
that were brought by the peace party Federalists against
the last war, to denounce it as an unrighteous, unholy,
and damnable war; to hold up our government to the
eyes of the world as the aggressors in the conflict; to
charge it with motives of conquest and aggrandizement;
to parade and portray in the darkest colors all the hor-
rors of war; to dwell upon its cost and depict its ca-
lamities.'

" Now, that was the doctrine of Judge Thurman as
to the duties of citizens in time of war — in time of
such a war as the Mexican war even, in which no vital
interest of the country could by possibility suffer.
Judge Thurman says that General Hayes, in his speech,

has a great many slips cut from the newspapers, and that he must have had some sewing society of old ladies to cut out the slips for him. I don't know how he found that out. I never told it, and you know the ladies never tell secrets that are confided to them. I hold in my hand a speech of Judge Thurman, from which I have read extracts, and I find that he has in it slips cut from more than twenty different prints, sermons, newspapers, old speeches, and pamphlets, to show how, in the war of 1812, certain Federalists uttered unpatriotic sentiments. I presume he must have acquired his slips on that day in the way he says I acquired mine now.

" Now, my friends, I propose to hold Judge Thurman to no severe rule of accountability for his conduct during the war. I merely ask that it shall be judged by his own rule : ' Your country is engaged in war, and it is the duty of every citizen to say nothing and do nothing which shall depress the spirits of his own countrymen, nothing that shall encourage the enemies of his country, or give them moral aid or comfort.' That is the rule. Now, Judge Thurman, how does your conduct square with it? I do not propose to begin at the beginning of the war, or even just before the war, to cite the record of Judge Thurman. I am willing to say that perhaps men might have been mistaken at that time. They might have supposed in the beginning a conciliatory policy, a non-coercive policy, would in some way avert the threatened struggle. But I ask you to approach the period when the war was going on, when armies to the number of hundreds of thousands of men were ready on one side and the other, and when the whole world knew what was the nature of the great struggle going on in America. Taking the beginning of 1863, how stands the conflict? We have pressed the rebellion out of Kentucky and through Tennessee. Grant stands before Vicksburg, held at bay by the army of Pembertòn; Rosecrans, after the capture of Nashville, has pressed forward to Murfreesboro', but is still held out of East Tennessee by the army of Bragg. The army of the Potomac and the army of Lee, in Virginia, are balanced, the one against the other. The whole world knows that that exhausting struggle cannot last long without deciding in favor of one side or the other. That the year 1863 is big with the fate of Union and of liberty, every intelligent man in the world knows — that on one side it is a struggle for nationality and human rights. There is not in all Europe a petty despot who lives by grinding the masses of the people, who does not know that Lincoln and the Union are his enemies. There is not a friend of freedom in all Europe who does not know that Lincoln and the loyal army are fighting in the cause of free government for all the world. Now, in that contest, where are you, Judge Thurman? It is a time when we need men and money, when we need to have our people inspired with hope and confidence. Your sons and brothers are in the field. Their success depends upon your conduct at home.

" The men who are to advise you what to do have

upon them a dreadful responsibility to give you wise
and patriotic advice. Judge Thurman, in the speech I
am quoting from, says : —

" ' But now, my friends, I shall not deal with obscure
newspapers or obscure men. What a private citizen
like Allen G. Thurman may have said in 1861 is a
matter of indifference.'

" Ah, no, Judge Thurman, the Union party does not
propose to allow your record to go without investigation because you are a private citizen. I know you
held no official position under the government at the
time I speak of ; but, sir, you had for years been a
leading, able, and influential man in the great party
which had often carried your State. You were acting
under grave responsibilities. More than that, during
that year, 1863, you were more than a private citizen.
You were one of the delegates to the State convention
of that year ; you were one of the committee that
forms your party platform in that convention ; you
were one of the central committee that carries on the
canvass in the absence of your standard-bearers ; and
you were one of the orators of the party. No, sir,
you were not a private citizen in 1863. You were
one of the leading and one of the ablest men in your
party in that year, speaking through the months of
July, August, September, and October, in behalf of the
candidate of the peace party. You cannot escape as a
private citizen.

" Well, sir, in the beginning of that eventful year,
there rises in Congress the ablest member of the peace

party, to advise Congress and to advise the people, and
what does he say?

"'You have not conquered the South. You never
will. It is not in the nature of things possible, especially under your auspices. Money you have expended
without limit; blood you have poured out like water.'

"Now, mark the taunt — the words of discourage-
ment that were sent to the people and to the army of
the Union : —

"'Defeat, debt, taxation, sepulchres, these are your
trophies. Can you get men to enlist now at any
price?'

"Listen again to the words that were sent to the
army and to the loyal people : —

"'Ah, sir, it is easier to die at home.'

"We knew that, Judge Thurman, better than Mr.
Vallandigham knew it. We had seen our comrades
falling and dying alone on the mountain side and in the
swamps — dying in the prison-pens of the Confederacy
and in the crowded hospitals, North and South. Yet
he had the face to stand up in Congress, and say to the
people and the world, 'Ah, sir, it is easier to die at
home.' Judge Thurman, where are you at this time?
He goes to Columbus to the State convention, on the
11th of June of that year, in all the capacities in which
I have named him — as a delegate, as committee-man,
and as an orator — and he spends that whole summer
in advocating the election of the man who taunted us
with the words, 'Defeat, debt, taxation, sepulchres,
these are your trophies.'"

Was it Mr. Thurman, or was it really Mr. Tilden whom General Hayes meant? And is it really of Mr. Thurman that he goes on to speak?

" This, my friends, is a part of that record which we are invited to examine by my friend, Judge Thurman. I ask you to apply to it *the principle that whoever, during the great struggle, was unfaithful to the cause of the country is not to be trusted to be one of the men to harvest and secure the legitimate fruits of the victory which the Union people and the Union army won during the rebellion. . . .*

" It is not worth while now to consider, or undertake to predict, when we shall cease to talk of the records of those men. It does seem to me that it will for many years to come be the voice of the Union people of the State that for a man who as a leader — as a man having control in political affairs — that for such a man, who has opposed the interests of his country during the war, ' the post of honor is the private station.' When shall we stop talking about it? When ought we to stop talking about that record, when leading men come before the people? Certainly not until every question arising out of the rebellion, and every question which is akin to the questions which made the rebellion, is settled. Perhaps these men will be remembered long after these questions are settled; perhaps their conduct will long be remembered. What was the result of this advice to the people? It prolonged the war; it made it impossible to get recruits; it made it necessary that we should have drafts. They opposed the drafts, and that made rioting, which required that troops should be called from all the armies in the field to preserve the peace at home. From forty to a hundred thousand men in the different States of this Union were kept within the loyal States to perserve the peace at home. And now, when they talk to you about the debt and about the burden of taxation, remember how it happened that the war was so prolonged, that it was so expensive, and that the debt grew to such large proportions."

As a politician, in the sense of a successful candidate for office, Hayes has been, as Mr. Lowell says of Lincoln, "wise without a plan." His only schemes, practiced after he came to power, have been for the public advantage. How to come to power never gave him an hour's unrest. It would be idle to pretend that such a man has not felt honored by the honors done him; he is neither so ungrateful, so obtuse, nor so arrogant as not to have deeply felt them; but he has always felt that honesty was better than honor, and he has never sought the one at the cost of the other; he has asked no favors and has used no arts.

As a public orator, a speaker for occasions, Hayes has little of the ready eloquence that goes to the making of a brilliant speech. His political and legal arguments strike us as far better, with their weighty and solid movement, their stalwart grace, their deep conviction just touched and not more than touched with poetry. Yet even in those slighter efforts in which he does not shine, he satisfies with his sense and serious fitness. Here, for example, is a little speech made at the dedication of the beautiful Davidson fountain in Cincinnati : —

" FELLOW CITIZENS, — It is altogether fitting that the citizens of Cincinnati should feel a deep interest in the occasion which has called together this large assemblage. It is well to do honor to this noble gift, and to do honor to the generous giver. This work lends a new charm to the whole city.

" Longfellow's lines in praise of the Catawba that grows on the banks of the Beautiful River give to the Catawba a finer flavor, and render the Beautiful River still more beautiful. When art and genius give to us in marble or on canvas the features of those we admire or love, ever afterward we discover in their faces and in their characters more to admire and more to love.

" This work makes Cincinnati a pleasanter city, her homes more happy, her aims worthier, and her future brighter.

" But this fountain does not pour out its blessings for Cincinnati, or for her visitors and guests alone. Cincinnati is one of the central cities of the nation — of the great continent. It is becoming the convention city. Witness the national assemblies in the interest of commerce, of industry, of education, of benevolence, of progress, of religion, which annually gather here from the most distant parts of America. This monument is an instructor of all who come. Whoever beholds it will carry away some part of the lesson it teaches. The duty which the citizen owes to the community in which and by which he has prospered, that duty this work will forever teach. No rich man who is wise will, in the presence of this example, willingly go to his grave with his debt to the public unpaid and unprovided for. Many a last will and testament will have a beneficent codicil, suggested by the work we inaugurate to-day. Parks, fountains, schools, galleries of art, libraries, hospitals, churches, whatever benefits and elevates mankind, will here receive much needed encouragement and support.

"This work says to him who, with anxious toil and care, has successfully gathered and hoarded, Do not neglect your great opportunity. Divide wisely and equitably between the few who are most nearly of your own blood, and the many who in kinship are only a little farther removed. If you regard only those reared under your own roof, your cherished estate will soon be scattered, perhaps wasted by profligate heirs in riotous living, to their own ruin, and you and your fortune will quickly be forgotten. Give a share, pay a tithe, to your more distant and more numerous kindred — to the general public, and you will be gratefully remembered, and mankind will be blessed by your having lived!

"Many, reflecting on the uncertainty of the future, will prefer to see their benefactions distributed and applied while they are still living. Regarding their obligations to the public as sacred debts, they will wish to pay as they go. This is commendable. Perhaps it is safest.

"But at some time and somehow the example here

presented will and must be followed. All such deeds are the parents of other similar good deeds. And so the circle within which the blessings flowing from this fountain are enjoyed will forever grow wider and wider, and the people of distant times and places will rejoice to drink, as we now do, healthful and copious draughts in honor of its founder."

A far nobler effort, one that has deeply impressed us with the strange qualities of its power, is the address which Hayes delivered at the dedication of a soldiers' monument in Findlay, Ohio, last year. Here, perhaps more strongly than anywhere else, his manner has reminded us of that of Lincoln; yet Lincoln's eloquence had much more of the oratorical movement. In this singularly touching speech of Hayes's, there is no art. It is almost as helpless in this respect as the utterance of some able, slow-languaged Englishman. The diction in the most pathetic passages is plain and blunt almost to uncouthness; yet word by word the speaker draws nearer to you till, as if in the silence of the pathos-stricken crowd, you seem to hear the very throbbing of his heart. It is the supreme triumph of pure and deep feeling that will have none but the simplest expression.

"I know not," he said, speaking of the fallen soldiers, "how many of them have been gathered into the cemeteries near their home; I know not how many others have been gathered into the beautiful national cemeteries near the great battle-fields; I know not how many are lying in swamps, along the mountain-sides.

in nameless graves, the unknown heroes of the Union: but wherever they are, and however many there may be, you people of Hancock County have erected your monument to all who fell, who left your county. All soldiers, I am sure, feel like thanking you for this. I remember well that one of the saddest days of my life was after one of our great battles in the early period of the war. Recovering from wounds, with other comrades who had been wounded there, we passed near the battle-field, as soon as we felt able to do so ; and, when we came there, what did we learn ? Passing up the mountain, charging the line of the enemy, they fell ; and everywhere were the shallow graves in which were deposited the remains of our seven hundred companions who had fallen. And how were they buried ? and how was their last resting-place marked ? Hastily, tenderly, no doubt, the parties detailed to bury them had gathered up their remains. You soldiers know how it was done. They placed upon the face of each man who died, whenever they could ascertain his name, a piece of an envelope, or a scrap of a letter, or something of the kind, containing his name, his company, his regiment, fastening it there, hoping that some day his friends might come and find him, and learn who was there buried. And then, you remember, there were no coffins, nothing of the sort ; but they took the blue overcoat, and placed it around the man, and took the cape, and, bringing it over the face, fastened it down. This was his shroud ; this was his coffin ; and he was placed away to rest until the resurrection morn. That was the manner of his burial. And strange, I may say, was the result of that woollen material over the face: saturated with water, and covered with the earth, it did so protect them from decay, that months afterwards many were recognized by their friends, preserved as they were by the overcoat cape. And how was the grave marked? With a pencil they scratched upon a piece of pine board — a thin piece of cracker-box — the name and company, which was placed at the grave. This was all then; and we did not know what the result would be. We did not know what friends would do, what monuments would be reared.

"As we left that field, talking to each other, we said there must be a soldiers' monument for the soldiers of our regiment. I would not claim that this was the first regiment that built a monument; that the twenty-third Ohio, to which I had the honor to belong, built the first monument: but I will say it was the first I heard of. After the famous Antietam campaign was fought, we called the men together, — four hundred and fifty or five hundred men, — and from the scanty pay which was to support the men, and to some extent their families, the majority of the remainder subscribed at least one dollar, and others more, according to their ability, and raised in the regiment two thousand dollars to build a monument, on which, it was agreed, should be inscribed the name of every man in the regiment who had fallen, and every man who should fall during the continuance of the war. We had it placed in the cemetery at Cleveland, where more of our number came from than from any other place. Many a monument has been built since, far grander than that, taller, and finer, and more expensive; but that, so far as I know, was the first soldiers' monument.

"We are glad to know that you of Hancock County have not neglected your duty in that regard. You mean that those men shall have their monument, and be remembered forever. It will be a monument that will have its value to you and your children. It will be an instructor, a teacher of lessons to all who look on it. What is it? Why did these men perish? Why was this monument built? Here is a great nation: here is a country stretching from ocean to ocean, over the finest part of the best continent on the globe. On the day that they volunteered, the only enemy that the American nation could know, could fear, could dread, was in war against us. We cared nothing for foreign nations; they were too far, too distant; and anyway, with the North and South united, as I believe they now are, in feeling, we can meet the world in arms against us. A house divided against itself — there was the danger; and that was the danger that these men went out to meet. And now, how is it to-day? How stands the matter now? We know every acre of that beautiful land belongs only to the stars and stripes, and belongs to the flag forever.

"And not only that lesson does it teach; but it teaches, also, that this Union is dedicated to the principles of the Declaration of Independence. I hardly know what others may think about that; but I believe

that in fifty years past there never was a time when
there was that prospect of complete and enduring harmony among all classes of people, in all sections of this
country, that there is to-day. Why, think of it! On
the 17th of June, the hundredth anniversary of the
battle of Bunker Hill, we had Maryland Confederate
regiments and soldiers saluting — in the streets of Boston, and on Boston Common and Bunker Hill — the
men of Massachusetts: we had South Carolina and
Massachusetts shoulder to shoulder, as in the days
when their fathers beat the British a hundred years
ago. All this, I think, is due, in a great measure,
to the success of our men to whom this monument is
erected, and their comrades in other States and other
organizations, living and dead. Think of the men
themselves who were there, — citizen soldiers, not one,
perhaps, of whom, was ever acquainted with war, or
ever bred to war. Here and there one had been in the
Mexican war; here and there one had been in some
Indian war; but, as a rule, they all came from civil
life: they all came from where they were sovereigns,
to be, for three years, obedient to men who were not
better than themselves.

" Why, they tell us our bayonets could think. Yes,
and often and often it was the glory, in my judgment,
of the private soldier that the bayonet thought more
truly, more wisely, more accurately, than the sword.
A celebrated English statesman said, ' I can understand
why these Americans, to the number of millions, rushed
to arms to defend the government they had made.

There is no mystery in that. Now, I do not understand how it was, that, at the end of that war, a million of men quietly disbanded, and returned to the walks of peaceful life, and went back about their old occupations, and became again good citizens.' There was one great advantage we had, — a people so educated, and so intelligent in all classes, that we could raise an army of that sort.

"Our monument, then, stands and teaches us of the importance of the Union, the importance of the principles of the Declaration of Independence, and the importance of universal education. My friends, what is a monument, however costly and beautiful, if it does not teach us some of the duties of practical life, how the living shall deal with the living? When you shall see the widows of the soldiers, the parents and orphans of the soldiers, every man whose heart is in the right place feels his sympathies warmed towards them. There is no doubt as to that, I am sure, in any Christian community. But there is another lesson. The men who fell, the men who lost an arm or leg, the widows and orphans who are left, are not the only victims of the war. There must always be another class. We rejoice to know that the great body of young men who went out to the war returned to their homes, more manly, braver, and better than when they left them, but they were gone, many of them, at the critical period of life, from sixteen to twenty years of age, just the period when they must learn habits of thrift, and the knowledge of occupations and trades that shall enable them to get

that independence which every man in America ought
to have or try to have. They were during that period
in the army ; and some came back with habits to which
we regret to allude. But, my friends, when we look at
that monument, we should be reminded that that man
who may have thus formed any pernicious habits in the
army is always one of the victims of the war. He has
lost that which is better than life in trying to save the
republic. Avert not your gaze, patriotic men, from
that man. Lift him up, help him, never give him up.
Give him occupation, give him good words ; save him, if
you can. At any rate, treat him as one of the victims
of the war."

What Hayes was as a soldier, the reader can best
learn from his history in the war — a history only too
slightly and inadequately sketched in these pages. To
his regiment he was one of the good colonels, and to his
brigade one of the good generals, looking to the comfort, the health, the honor, and the morality of his men
with literally the same studied care, the same enlightened vigilance, that a father bestows upon his children ;
and in return he enjoyed from them a devotion that
knew no limit ; wherever he led they followed ; whatever he said they did. A private of the twenty-third,
writing of his colonel, says : " A braver or better man
was not in the army. He had an abundance of grit.
If he had a fault, it was that in battle he was too eager.
On a long, dusty march I could always tell Colonel
Hayes's horse, as it was always loaded with the guns
and knapsacks of ' the boys ' who were giving out, the

colonel himself walking by its side, no matter how great
the heat. Yes, sir, he was a kind man, but we had to
do our whole duty as soldiers."

When he was removed from the command of the first
brigade, " The boys looked upon you," wrote one of his
officers, " more in the light of a father than a military
commander, and while we all regret that old associations must be broken off, yet we feel assured that whatever station you may be called upon to fill in the future,
you will acquit yourself with like honors to those now
attending you as the commander of the old first brigade."

The testimony of officers and those competent to
judge of his professional qualities as a soldier, is of but
one effect. "In military life," writes General Comly,
who served under him throughout the war, and was
himself a soldier of heroic temper and achievement,
" he was noted among army men for his coolness, firmness, and daring. No emergency ever came upon him
that he was not equal to. The West Point men regarded him as one of the very best officers in the volunteer service, and attributed to him a very high order
of military genius. His courage, though of the most
undemonstrative sort, was absolutely sublime, and was
attested by three or four wounds received in the very
front of battle. His charge at Winchester, where he
led his brigade through a deep slough in the face of
the enemy, plunging his horse into the mire up to the
saddle-bow, and being the first man over, though a perfect storm of bullets swept about him, was scarcely ex-

celled during the whole war as a feat of personal daring.   Yet this was but one incident of a dozen similar ones in his army career that might be named. Had he been as clamorous for promotion, and as impatient for popular appreciation as some officers were, he would have been placed at the head of a corps, or one of the grand armies, instead of a division."

Not only do Grant, Sherman, Sheridan, and all the other great Ohio soldiers of West Point education, or of native military genius developed in the volunteer service, esteem and praise his soldiership, but wherever scientific soldiers of Eastern origin came in contact with him they acknowledged his capacity and power. We have just been shown a private letter from a New England officer, a general of volunteers in West Virginia, a graduate of West Point, and now holding very high rank in the regular army, who speaks of Hayes in terms no less cordial and unstinted than these : —

" September 4, 1876.

" I am glad to assure you, not only of my full and undoubted conviction of the success of General Hayes, but still more the further conviction that from week to week comes over me, that he as fully *merits* that success.   And though I was not so much brought in contact with him as if he had been in my own brigade, I recollect very distinctly his quiet, unobtrusive, gentlemanly manner, and his faithful attention to duty in the West Virginia campaign, from Carnifex Ferry to its close. *It was of the same type exactly with the modest worth and quiet, reserved power of Grant and of Thomas,* since so well known to the country. . . . . I firmly believe his administration is to be our *political* and *national* salvation.

" I have always felt that the daily letters, the record of events written at the time by those engaged in them, were the most valuable papers ever to be had, either as to the truth of the events or to show the characters of the writers ; and I doubt not the most interesting and important articles for the *national* (I do not call it political) contest now coming on will be those which give most fully the very words and thoughts of the moment (as the great events of the war were passing), of this brave, honest man, whom the people will delight to honor, as his fellow soldiers now do; this modest Bayard, in war or in peace — as the whole country finds, and will ever find — *sans peur et sans reproche.*"

It is superfluous to multiply these testimonies, as we might to any extent, from rank and file alike. They are as unanimous — a hater of Aristides might say as monotonous — as the witnesses to the purity, efficiency, and economy of Hayes's civil administrations. What his character as a congressman was, we have already seen ; and as governor of a great State we have allowed him to speak for himself in extracts from his messages. On some points he was necessarily silent. He could not say what we know from examination of his letters and diaries, that his smallest official act followed only upon the most careful and conscientious deliberation. His appointments have been made after the closest possible inquiry into the character and qualifications of the persons appointed; and no fault has been found with them except by Republicans who have blamed him for the impartiality with which he has named Democrats for places in which he judged that purely partisan appointments might be to the public disadvantage. We have yet to know of a single instance in which that eminent civil service reformer, Mr. Tilden, has laid himself open to reproach by giving office to a political opponent.

As governor, Hayes has conceived it his business to attend to State affairs, and only to notice national questions as they concern citizens of Ohio. He has not been putting out feelers for the presidency, nor manufacturing a reputation on which he could lift himself into partisan prominence; and he has not, like Governor Tilden, lugged into his messages the discussion of every sort of irrelevant affair. He has applied himself closely to the study of the sources of Ohio's prosperity, and probably no man in the State knows them so well as he. A gentleman who recently talked with him on such matters confessed his astonishment at the extent and minuteness of his knowledge relating to the agriculture, manufactures, and mines of the State; but Hayes seemed to think it was part of his duty, as the first citizen, to be second to none in this knowledge.

He has not only bestowed unusual attention upon the condition of the asylums and prisons, but he has been extremely careful in the exercise of the pardoning power, which he has used according to principles arrived at through diligent study of the results in cases coming within his own experience or observation. Inclining always towards mercy, he has suffered no personal feeling to cloud his judgment in such matters, and in more public affairs, involving disturbances of order or violations of law, he has acted with instant vigor. His promptness in quelling the riots of the striking coal-miners in Ohio, during the present year, is an earnest of what his action would be on a larger theatre in any greater emergency, and the following letter to his adjutant-general, who was sent with troops to crush out the riots, shows the temper of a ruler not disposed to dally with his duty, or to address a murderous mob as his " friends."

DEAR GENERAL, — I still feel that there is doubt as to the sufficiency of your force. Be sure to have it ample. If you call out too many men, I will be responsible, but if you fail for want of enough, it will be your fault. It now looks as if this trouble would last a long time. I wish you to make preparations to hold your men in camp near Massillon, until all danger from lawless violence is at an end ; therefore let your arrangements be of a more permanent character ; let it be understood that you mean to stay until lawlessness ceases, or is plainly controllable by the civil authorities. Sincerely yours, R. B. HAYES.

" Hayes's capacity for civil affairs," says a journalist of the State which knows him best, " has been

severely tested, and the tests have developed executive
abilities of the very highest order.   With a rare knowledge of men and affairs, he has shown a genius for
doing the right thing in the right way and at the right
time.   In prudence, moderation, and sturdy good sense,
he bears a striking resemblance to Abraham Lincoln,
as he does also in his simplicity, and keen, almost un-
erring sagacity.   Few men have, with such caution,
such strength of will and power of decision."

Not more, but not less valuable than the praise of an
impartial friend, is that of an impartial enemy, and Mr.
Dana, of the "New York Sun," may now speak for
the man whose defeat he desires : —

"Hayes is a man of talent; he is a gentleman ; he
is rich and independent ; he served with credit as a
soldier in the war, *and his record as governor of Ohio
is without flaw or spot.*"

Of Hayes as a citizen and a man, what remains to be
said ?   Nothing truly that will not make him even more
hateful to those already weary of hearing Aristides
called just.   Some of his moral and intellectual qualities have been admirably given by an old acquaintance
of his in a letter printed by "The Nation."   "He is
not a 'magnetic' man; he is not audacious, he is not a
'leader,' he does not impress one as a great force, and
all that.   But when he has a duty to perform he first
proceeds to throw aside all nonsense, and, with a peculiar singleness and simplicity, sees just what the matter
is.   After that, the devil can't scare him.   I never
knew a man who listened with a franker willingness to

learn, and I have known very few men who were so
sure to end with an opinion of their own, which nothing
could shake. I observe that the little people of the
'Herald' and 'World' speak of him as a 'colorless'
candidate. Well, his color is not loud, but what they
actually mean is nonsense. They had better encounter
him some time when he has a duty to perform, and try
to turn him aside, and then tell us whether he has color.
I have seen him tried, and noticed that his color was a
good deal like steel. . . . . I need say nothing about
his honesty; you 've seen that mentioned by every
paper that names him, though perhaps I had as well
add that he is just absolute integrity. My main purpose was to speak of his capabilities, since that must be
the chief point of curiosity just now. For whatever it
is worth, my clear conviction is that he is a very able
man, very well informed, of a good deal of culture, of
rare soundness of judgment, and of a courageous and
high character."

Mr. Henry B. Blackwell, a friend of equally long
standing with the writer of the foregoing, has published
his impressions of Hayes's character in a letter to the
"Boston Advertiser," from which we transcribe a few
passages : —

" Mr. Hayes has a calm, cool, intellectual temperament, which is not easily roused, but which when
roused, moves promptly and with singular precision.
He has a clear, judicial intellect. He is not want-
ing in enthusiasm, but he never gushes. There is a
certain magnanimity, a stately and dignified repose of

character, which underlies his frank and genial temper, and which keeps his generous impulses from running away with him.   He is always and everywhere
a gentleman.   During our six or seven years of weekly
meetings,[1] I never knew him to use a harsh or coarse
expression, nor ever knew him to indulge in a personality.   He never made an enemy, nor lost a friend.
Nothing sordid or selfish was ever associated with his
character.   Always cheerful, kind, frank, and sympathetic, he took a keen interest in every question,
and occasionally spoke, when roused, effectively and to
the purpose.   But he seldom was roused to speak except in conversation.   There he was always ready,
bright, and animated.   It was a common remark in
those days, at the club, ' Hayes is capable of rising to
any distinction, if he could only be impelled to seek it.'
But he seemed totally devoid of personal ambition, and
unwilling to take any of the ordinary steps to attain notoriety ; yet this very coolness and indifference to per
sonal aggrandizement has proved the secret of his subsequent political success.   He has never sought position.
He has never lifted his hand to become a candidate for
any place.   The office has always sought the man, not
the man the office."

   Some reminiscences, sketchily jotted down by an old
friend of Hayes's college days, and kindly transferred
to the present writer by Mr. J. Q. Howard, for whose
careful work[2] they came too late, present traits of

---

[1] In the Cincinnati Literary Club.
[2] Life of Rutherford B. Hayes.   (Robert Clarke & Co., Cincinnati.)

the man too essential to a good portrait to be lost. We think the reader will enjoy these all the better, if given without our manipulation. "Hayes was the champion in college, in debate class section, and in the foot-path; cheerful, sanguine, and confident of the future, never seeing cause for desponding; was a young man of substantial physique; in my whole acquaintance, I never knew of his being sick one day, and so free from any weakness as to seem indefatigable. His greatest amusements were fishing and chess. In company he was humorous to hilarity, told quick, pungent stories, many of which I remember with laughter to this day; took things as they came; used to laugh at the shape of our boarding-house roast beef, but still ate.

"I grew from boyhood, knowing him as a good friend, to whom I went whenever too lazy to study, or foundered by my problems, and I always found help and good cheer. Do not think he had many *intimate* friends; those with whom he was intimate were, and are now, the best men of my acquaintance. I don't remember a single man with whom he was intimate but that has been successful in his vocation, showing that Hayes either had an intuitive disgust for mean spirits and rejected them, or else changed them. He had all the appearance of a fighting man, and I think in all college scrimmages was let alone. Have often heard it said that he 'did nothing for his friends;' perhaps not, but his real friends generally needed no help, or were not of that class who attached themselves for selfish interests. Even in his political labors, I am sure he never entangled himself by promises or by such intimacies as to bind him, but never shrank from tackling any subject or measure of policy when brought to him. He never walked around anything, but took it by the horns and shook it, or was shaken. I think him a square specimen of an Anglo-Saxon, honest man; stubbornly square in his views; of simple ideas of life; that is, he had such ideas as would make him prefer heaping, round measure of good to pretension and false appearances.

" The independence of his character was shown on commencement day at Kenyon. He was valedictorian, and I remember how grand he looked in my boy eyes because he was n't able to have splendid new clothes, and was independent enough to do without. That was the first impression made on my mind, evidencing a pure, thorough self-sacrifice. I was but sixteen years old, and think I see him now, with what we knew then as a box-coat with side pockets, when all the rest were dressed in new black cloth frock-coats.

"I spent the summer of 1844 with him at Cambridge, Mass., as a law student; I as an amateur (i. e. a listener who never studies), he as a regular student. He then showed himself thoroughly independent of everything and everybody. Judge Story always noticed him especially, as he came into the lecture room. In the practice of law his advice was always against litigation. When offered the city solicitorship, we talked it over, and I urged him to take it for its introduction to the public. He always refused to do anything to advance his own interests; but, don't try to make him a saint; he was n't; he was nothing but a good honest specimen of a man.

"Three months ago I wrote to him about his presidential prospects, and his reply was emphatically, 'I cannot do anything to aid myself.' And on June 7, 1876, he writes, 'I am luckily constituted, or the things you allude to would be vexations; the truth is, I am in no way complicated, entangled, or committed with the parties you name, or anybody else.' And I believe if he is elected President of the United States, *no man ever went into office so free from obligations as he will be.* The head-quarters of the Hayes movement in this section during the campaign were projected by his personal friends; not one cent was contributed by an office-holder or politician."

It was a good usage of the old-fashioned biographers, with whom we would fain ally ourselves in some sort, to delineate the persons of their heroes; and the reader, we hope, would not be content without some such picture of Hayes. The material for such a picture is vast enough, but the authorities upon his looks are not so well agreed as those upon his morals. In its way, a sketch by Judge Johnston, in an address to a ratification meeting at Avondale, Ohio, is, we are told, quite trustworthy: —

"Place him on a platform together with one hundred distinguished men, and call in an able connoisseur, who has neither seen nor heard of any one of them, and he will point him out as a model man; neither too large nor too small, nor too tall nor too short, nor too fat nor too lean, nor too old nor too young. A man in the prime and vigor of healthful manhood, with blood in his veins and marrow in his bones; able to endure any labor, either of body or of mind, which may devolve upon him. His face seems made to match his form. No painful, care-worn wrinkles, indicative of infirmities or misfortunes, to provoke a grudge against nature, or engender sourness toward mankind. Nor does he wear a smirking face, as if he were a candidate for admiration; but a fine, sunny countenance, such as men and women respect, and children love. His manners, like his countenance, are simple and sincere. He don't run to meet you, and call you '*My* VERY DEAR *sir:*' He takes you by the hand, with a cordial kindness which recognizes the universal brotherhood of man, and impresses you that he is a man who gets above nobody, and nobody gets above him."

If this is not enough, there is a yet closer portraiture — also said to be faithful — by Mr. Keenan, writing for one of the Chicago newspapers. It is well to premise that Hayes's complexion is of the true Scotch sandiness, and that his once tawny beard and hair are both now touched with gray. "His complexion," says Mr. Keenan, "has the ripe tinge of health. He is much in the open air, and has cheeks like a reaper's — fresh, brown, and thickly bearded. He has no gift of music evidently, for his bright, frank, blue eyes are set closely together, under a fair, clear, shapely forehead. The nose is a column of strength, if physiognomy's laws are to be trusted. It is not the hooked beak of the Cæsars, but the complex formation which marks the stronger type of the Anglo-Saxons. The lower face, where the lines can be seen, is symmetrical, strong, and reassuring. In repose or animation the face is a fine one."

And now that we stand, as it were, in the very presence of the man, let him speak once more for himself, and let his final utterances be those magnanimous words which are truest to his broad and generous nature. Here is a letter written home in the very midst of the Shenandoah Valley campaign, which we commend to the perusal of the whole country, North and South : —

"CHARLESTON, CAMP ELK, *July* 2, 1864.

"You wrote one thoughtless sentence, complaining of Lincoln for failing to protect our unfortunate prisoners by retaliation. All a mistake! all such things should be avoided as much as possible. *We* have done too much rather than too little. You use the phrase 'brutal rebels.' Don't be cheated in that way. There are enough 'brutal rebels,' no doubt, but there are plenty of humane rebels. I have seen a good deal of it on our late trip. War is cruel business, and there is brutality in it on all sides, but it is very idle to get up anxiety on account of any supposed peculiar cruelty on the part of rebels."

The man who could feel so justly towards enemies from whom he was in daily, hourly peril, wrote home yet one other letter which we must give to show how tolerantly he could feel toward one consenting to represent a cause which he abhorred: —

"CAMP SUMMIT POINT, VIRGINIA, *September* 9, 1864.

" Speaking of politics, it is quite common for youngsters, adopting their parents' notions, to get very bitter talk into their innocent little mouths. I was quite willing W. [his son] should 'hurrah for ——,' last summer with the addition, 'and a rope to hang him,' but I feel quite different about McClellan. He is on a mean platform, and is in bad company; but I do not doubt his personal loyalty; and he has been a soldier, and what is more, a soldier's friend. No man ever treated the private soldier better. No commander was ever more loved by his men. I therefore want my boys taught to think and talk well of General McClellan."

This, then, is our leader. The proportions are heroic, but the figure is not larger than life; and the nearer we draw to it, the more august and benign are the lineaments. A scholar, and a lover of letters and the arts; fine by nature and refined by culture, careful self-study, and wide knowledge of both men and books; a soldier of dauntless bravery and approved genius; a statesman and public servant of the best principles and of irreproachable performance, his highest commendation to our honor and our trust is still that he is a true and good man.

Among the escutcheons of the old Scottish borderers which hang on the walls of Sir Walter Scott's library, at Abbotsford, are those of the Rutherfords and the Hayeses. The arms of the Hayeses are a shield with a Greek cross and four stars, surmounted by a dove, and having for legend one word — a word which has always been the instinct and the principle of the man whose life we have so imperfectly portrayed —

" RECTE ! "

SKETCH OF THE LIFE

OF

WILLIAM A. WHEELER.

SKETCH OF THE LIFE

OF

WILLIAM A. WHEELER.

———◆———

THE writer of this sketch, though counting himself among the friends of Mr. Wheeler, does not feel at liberty to indulge in mere eulogy of him, regarding him only from the standpoint of personal friendship. The attitude of Mr. Wheeler as a candidate for one of the highest offices in the gift of the people, gives them a right to exact and impartial information respecting both his public career and his personal character as bearing on the question of his fitness for the high position to which he has been named. For in this canvass, more perhaps than in any previous one, personal integrity as the surest guaranty of official rectitude, is emphasized beyond all other qualifications. And most happily both for Mr. Wheeler and the nation, the more both his public career and his personal character are known, the more deserving of the confidence of the people at this critical time, will he be proved. "Let them turn their calcium light on me," he said to one who rallied him on his calmness under public scrutiny just before the Convention, "they will find nothing which will make my friends ashamed of me." To this proud assertion of the consciousness of right, limiting itself to modest self-acquittal, may be added by those who know the man and have watched his career, that "the fiercest light which beats upon" a candidate can reveal in him only new traits to admire and new virtues to honor. And more: Mr. Wheeler's character is such that it not only endures this strong light, but needs it in order to be brought out into observation. Some men show to advantage in the shade of common-place events, but wilt under the glare of great responsibilities. Mr. Wheeler belongs to the class of men who are greatest on great occasions and under the stress of great demands. This sketch — the writer must stipulate with his readers that this be understood — will not do him justice; no written life can, because the best part of his life is as yet unrevealed. He has spoken many brave and wise words which have had their influence in shaping memorable events; but what he has done is greater than what he has said; and he is greater than all he has said and done. If the people confirm him in the position of leadership to which one of the great national parties has designated him, it will be found that he has still in reserve resources of greatness and goodness upon which neither his party nor the nation has yet drawn.

PARENTAGE.

Mr. Wheeler comes of good stock. Three great New England principles are traceable in the family for several generations: love of freedom, love of knowledge, and the fear of God. The grandfather Wheeler was in the first Concord fight. The maternal grandfather, William Woodward, was a soldier all through the Revolution. The Wheeler branch of the family, from Massachusetts, and the Woodward branch, from Connecticut, came together in Vermont, where Almon Wheeler, father of William, was born, and where he lived till two months before his son's birth. It thus appears that both the Republican candidates are of Vermont parentage. We may be permitted to hope that this fact is no bad omen either for the character of the men or the success of the candidates. Mr. Wheeler at least seems not to augur ill of his origin. "I have Vermont blood in my veins," he said at Montpelier, "and Vermont ideas in my head. My father was a Highgate man and my mother a Castleton woman, and in my early days I lived in the town of Fairfax, where under the shadow of old Fletcher Mountain, I learned from a valued uncle, in the intervals of the toil which was the common lot of almost all men in those days, those lessons which only the true New Englander could inculcate."

EDUCATION.

There runs through the Wheeler family the story, so common in New England families of those times, of struggles with poverty and hardship in the pursuit of education. In this case it was the old story in its most pathetic form, ambition saddened by ill health and arrested short of the hoped-for success.   Almon Wheeler, obliged by sickness to suspend his studies in the University of Vermont, at Burlington, entered upon the practice of law, in which he gave promise of eminence, but died at the early age of thirty-seven.   His son, William Almon, born at Malone, New York, June 30, 1819, was but eight years old at his father's death. For the support of the family, consisting of William and two sisters, the widowed mother found herself in possession of an estate valued at about $300, and encumbered by a mortgage.   But this mother, Eliza Woodward Wheeler, — her name deserves to be writ large,— was a woman of great force of character, concealed under the gentlest exterior.   By taking boarders for the academy at the rate of $1.25 a week, she contrived to keep her little family from want, and to give William the chance to attend the district schools until he was old enough to earn something for himself while pursuing his studies preparatory to college.   During this time he taught schools and "boarded round," in winters, and worked at farming in the laboring season, sometimes for months' wages, sometimes for the tenth bushel of corn husked, the tenth basket of potatoes dug, according to the custom of the region.   If ever his ambition flagged or his hope grew dim, in view of all that lay between him and the great prize of a liberal education, the mother's heroic spirit came to the rescue and helped him through the momentary lull of his own aspirations.   And as Providence would have it, in all this brave, patient, strenuous battle with the hardships of his life, the lad was not only knitting his physical and moral frame into condition for manly work, but was drawing the attention of many to himself as one whom they might well put in the way of promotion when the opportunity should come. At the age of nineteen, with a capital of $30 lent him by a former friend who had more faith in William than in himself, he entered the University of Vermont and pursued the course of study for two years, absent from the classes much of the time to work and teach. His college contemporaries speak of him as a good scholar, studious, thoughtful, and having a great many ideas of his own. At the end of two years, the family necessities and an affection of the eyes compelled him, though with great reluctance, to leave college. Mr. Wheeler did not, however, cease to be a student. He has always been a thoughtful reader of the best books, especially in English literature. His style and utterance are those of an educated man. The writer does not remember to have ever heard him misconstruct a sentence or mispronounce a word, and this is much to say of the most finished . scholar.

LEGAL PRACTICE.

Immediately on leaving college, Mr. Wheeler entered upon the study of law with Asa Hascall, a leading lawyer of Malone, and after four years' study, three of the seven years then required being remitted on account of his classical discipline, was admitted to the bar and "soon acquired," says a former legal brother, "an enviable position as a keen advocate and wise counsellor,

which brought him clients, friends, and competence."
A throat trouble which seriously interfered with his
practice as an advocate, finally compelled him to abandon the profession of the law, which he did in 1851.

LOCAL AND STATE OFFICES.

From his early manhood, Mr. Wheeler has held a
succession of offices, the variety and importance of which
attest the confidence of those who know him best.
During his early struggles to maintain himself and his
family, his neighbors seemed to have bestowed all
their offices on him, one after another, as fast as he grew
up to them. While studying law, he was made town
clerk, school commissioner, and school inspector. At
the first election under the Constitution of 1846, by
which the county judges and district attorneys were
made eligible by popular vote, Mr. Wheeler, who was a
pronounced Whig, was elected district attorney, and
his partner, a Democrat, was elected judge, on a Union
ticket, it being then the desire of both parties to keep
judicial elections free from party strifes. In 1849, and
again in 1850, Mr. Wheeler was elected by the Whigs
a member of the New York Assembly, and in 1859 and
1860, was State senator for his district. Although he
was always an active, and was at times an ardent party
man, and was outspoken in the advocacy of the measures he approved, it is the testimony alike of his
political friends and opponents, that he had a delicate
sense of official responsibility; that he was broad and
catholic in his sympathies and acts as a legislator; and

severely just in giving or refusing his great influence
to the many interests that appealed to him. This may
explain the high respect which he has always enjoyed
from men of all parties, and his singular exemption
from that partisan calumny which is the disgrace of
American politics.

How Mr. Wheeler felt toward those who had advanced him to so many honors is touchingly mani-
fested by an impromptu address made to them shortly
after his nomination to the Vice-Presidency, which we
give at length, because it fills in with warmer touches
our meagre outline of his early life, and shows in
what estimate he holds the mere honors and rewards
of office as compared with the esteem of good men and
the approbation of his own heart: —

TOWNSMEN AND FRIENDS: Of the many congratulations proffered me since my nomination by the Republican Convention for the second place in the government of the United States, none have so stirred me
and come so near my heart as yours. If this nomination be an honor — and who shall gainsay it? — it is
your honor and not mine; I am the simple instrument
through which it is reflected. For what am I, and
what have I, that I have not received from you? It
was in the early confidence of the people of Malone,
in their cheering words of encouragement, and in their
unwavering support, that the foundations of whatever
success I have achieved in life were laid. In boyhood, in manhood, and now that the sun of life is well

past the meridian, these have been, and are now, my
refuge and strength.

No honor, however exalted, shall ever dim my gratitude to those who extended to me the helping hand
in my early struggles, and who have honored me with
life-long trust and substantial acts of kindness. Nor
can the glare and glitter of life at the national capital,
or the blandishments and hollow arts of its society,
ever efface the simple tastes and early habits learned
by me from the New England pioneers of this goodly
town, to which I always return with renewed pleasure
and gratitude. How many of those pioneers whose
memory is hallowed by me, would, if they could speak,
this morning join in your congratulations !

From the people of Malone I received my first political recognition. Even before I had attained my
majority they made me clerk of the town, an office in
which I magnified myself more than in all the offices I
have since possessed, and whose pecuniary emoluments
— $30 for the year — for recording the estrays of the
town and the laying out of new roads, were of more
value to me than the thousands I have since attained.

And right here I want to say a word especially to
the young men, so many of whom I see before me —
a class in whom I always take the deepest interest,
and with whose efforts in life to achieve honorable success I am always in deep sympathy. It is said that
a fellow feeling makes us wondrous kind. There are
few phases in the struggles of the boy or young man
to make his way in life in which I have not had severe

experience. When, forty years ago, on a cold December morning, before the dawn of day, I emerged from the humble home which then stood upon the site from which I now address you, to make my way on foot through the falling snow to an adjoining town to teach my first district school at ten dollars a month, "half store pay;" and when, during that winter, in the progress of boarding around, in the chambers of the log houses, through the shrunken roof boards, I was literally a "star gazer," had any one predicted to me that at some future period of my life I should be nominated by a great party to the second office in the gift of forty millions of people, it would have been deemed stranger to me than any of the tales of the "Arabian Nights" which so stirred my boyish wonder. With an imagination naturally vivid, I built many air castles in those days, but this nomination was not among the structures. My nomination has this lesson for you, young men. In this beneficent people's government of ours, every man, without regard to the accidents of birth or fortune, is, with character, industry, and perseverance, the equal of every other man, and honest efforts to make an honorable name in life are sure of recognition and reward. And despite the hard things we say of the world, my own experience is that it never withholds a helping hand from a young man who shows an upright, stern determination to help himself. Doing this, though he fail of political distinction, he will obtain the respect and confidence of his fellow men, which is far better.

"Honor and shame from no condition rise;
    Act well your part, there all the honor lies."

To be selected from this great, imperial common-wealth as its exponent of that party whose achievements for liberty and unity, and for the advancement of the great cause of human brotherhood, have no parallel in the annals of the world, is an honor which ought to gratify any man's ambition. But it is an honor which comes to me unexpectedly, which I did not seek, and which I say in all frankness I did not desire. So long as I might remain in the public service my preference was to remain in the House of Representatives. But how utterly empty and meaningless is the honor to me, standing in the shadow of this desolate home, you all well know.

To the great tribunal of the American people, in which issue is again joined by the two great leading parties which divide the country, we can safely leave the argument and the verdict. In the meantime, however our party relations may be ruffled, I trust our personal relations may remain undisturbed. And when the verdict shall be rendered in November, we shall all, as good citizens, desiring only the prosperity of our common country, cheerfully acquiesce in it, whatever it may be. And whatever the result shall be as to myself, I shall hope to remain secure in your personal confidence. That is my highest purpose and ambition. And when, in obedience to universal and inevitable law, after the fitful fever of life, its weary wheels shall at last stand still, and I shall go to the rest which, thank God, beyond the conflicts and bereavements of this life "*remaineth*," I know I shall be followed by that charity with which our better nature covers the short-comings and imperfections of those who lay aside life's armor, and cross the flood to join the great, silent majority.

THE CONSTITUTIONAL CONVENTION.

In 1867 Mr. Wheeler was chosen one of the delegates at large to the Constitutional Convention of the State of New York. This body was one of the ablest ever assembled in the State, embracing a large number of such men as Wm. M. Evarts, George W. Curtis, Horace Greeley, Sanford E. Church, Ira Harris, Samuel J. Tilden, Edwards Pierrepont, representatives of the best legal, financial, and administrative talent of the Empire State. Over this imposing body Mr. Wheeler was called to preside by the highly complimentary vote of 100 over 49, no competitor receiving over 9 votes. He took no part in the debates, " having to undergo " as Mr. Erastus Brooks, his colleague, expressed it, " a severe ordeal for a man of ability, literally putting a padlock upon his mind, being unable in consequence of his position to mingle in the debates." In making up the committees of this body, with characteristic magnanimity he put leading Democrats into several important positions. " I came to the chair," said he in his closing speech, " with the single purpose of administering its duties fairly and impartially ; remembering that the trust confided to us was neither for majorities nor mi-

norities, but for all alike as citizens of a common State."
Some of his ultra Republican friends were at first of-
fended by this course of action, but afterward acknowledged both its justice and policy.

AS A PRESIDING OFFICER,

there can be no question that Mr. Wheeler would
bring preëminent ability to the position of President of
the Senate. His mental characteristics, his quick per-
ception of the real issue through all perplexities, his
promptness of utterance and action, his habit of impartial judgment, mark him out for a presiding officer.
The Senate of New York discovered his parliamentary
ability and chose him its speaker pro tempore. Speaking to a resolution of thanks tendered to the president
at the close of the Constitutional Convention, Mr. Sanford E. Church said: "I have had some experience in
deliberative bodies, and I can say without qualification
that for impartiality, fairness, and ability, I have never
seen a presiding officer excel the presiding officer of this
body." And to this high testimony Mr. George W.
Curtis added: "I shall carry from this Convention the
profoundest impression of the dignified deliberation
which is possible for gentlemen in a period of great
political excitement, but who are called together to ad-
minister a great public trust. As for the gentleman
who has presided over our deliberations, we shall all, I
am sure, to the latest hour of our lives, bear his image
in our memories, as that of a most able, a most urbane,
and most skillful officer."

IN CONGRESS.

Mr. Wheeler has sat as Representative in the thirty-seventh, forty-first, forty-second, forty-third, and forty-fourth Congresses. During most of this time, while he has been recognized as one of the leading men in Congress by those within, he has been one of the least conspicuous in the eyes of those without. He has been a working rather than a talking member. His oratory, which is vigorous and effective, has been devoted to advocating and defending measures which came from his committees. During his whole career he has never made a volunteer speech. Our constituencies are coming slowly to understand that the men who are the most valuable in Congress, the men who influence legislation most effectually, are those who work hard in committees, talk but seldom on the floor, and then with business-like point and directness. Mr. Wheeler belongs to this class. When ordinary men have confused and muddled a question beyond any apparent hope of a settlement, a few words of clear good sense from Mr. Wheeler often closes the dispute. He has also another method of influencing votes, which is quite effective, but does not seem to be emulated by aspiring Congressmen as much as might be wished. He keeps such a vigilant watch over measures in progress, and forms his opinions on them so honestly and carefully, that men who want to rely on a sound judgment, and who distrust their own, find out how Mr. Wheeler intends to vote, and act accordingly. He is thus a kind of legislative conscience to a considerable number of members. His standing with his political opponents is shown by his being unanimously selected in the Democratic caucus as a member of the Belknap Impeachment Committee. With regard to the measures in Congress by which so many fair names have been smirched, let his colleague, Hon. Robert H. Ellis, speak for him : —

"No inquiry has ever connected his name with any transaction depending in the most remote degree on his legislative action. When it was the fashion for all men to dabble in railroad stocks and bonds, and his own training might have induced him to invest in such securities, Mr. Wheeler never bought or sold a share of stock or a single bond in any of the Pacific roads. His experience on his local railroad would have rendered his services of rare value to any one of the great enterprises with which he was brought into contact; and the cases are many where legislators have by such relations been introduced to remunerative employment. Mr. Wheeler is free from even such imputation upon his disinterestedness.

"Other men have not accounted it an offense to use knowledge obtained by them as legislators as a basis for investments and business transactions. Such knowledge Mr. Wheeler often had, but his sense of right and his instincts of fair play forbade his taking any such advantage. He has served his country in Congress for ten years, without adding to the moderate competence with which he first went to Washington. With simple tastes, he has never been greedy of gain either for its own sake or the luxury it would buy. As a legislator, the thought never occurred to him that his influence could bring riches, and not the shadow of a stain rests on his name.

"In the last Congress he was chairman of the Committee on Commerce, and a member of the Committee on Appropriations, and in the present Congress he serves on the same committees. In these positions, he has never been self-asserting. His leadership has not been that of push; he has never sought notoriety. He has walked modestly in the path of duty, without self-seeking, and fearing no consequences."

ECONOMY IN EXPENDITURE.

A short specimen of Mr. Wheeler's style of speaking in Congress is here appended. Let the reader note the ring of sincerity in this plea for economy, and make his own contrasts.

"In presenting the regular appropriation bill for the support of the army for the next fiscal year, the committee on appropriations invite for it close attention and examination. Economy in public expenditure is now the profession of every lip; its practice is the universal, imperative demand of the hour. The time has passed, for a while at least, when millions of the public funds can, as at some former periods, flow safely through the open sluice-ways of legislation without careful consideration and critical scrutiny. The specter of renewed and increased taxation now haunts

every hamlet in the land, and upon us, as possessing
the power, and in the exercise of a wise prudence and
discretion, the people rely to beat back from their
homes the unwelcome reality.

"Probably there has been no period in our history
when the people were more sensitive upon the subject
of taxation, or more keenly inquisitive as to its necessity. The great and, until quite recently, steady reduction of our national indebtedness, and the removal
of the greater portion of the burdensome taxation im-
posed by the war, led our people to believe, with reason, that their long-fettered energies and industries
were at length unloosed, and the country once more
placed upon the sure road to permanent prosperity.
The sudden dissipation of these hopes surprises and
disheartens them, and all the more, as they are now
suffering from severe monetary derangements and the
great reduction of values ever, in time, inseparable
from an inflated paper currency.

"The people are now ill able and ill disposed to bear
burdens not demanded by palpable, immediate, pressing
necessity. They demand of us to practice here the
economy to which they are forced, and to bend to the
necessity which overpowers them.

"We ought now and here to accept and legislate for
the future upon the fact that certain great questions,
which have for the past few years overshadowed all
others, and to which, for the time, all others were
justly subordinated, have been substantially settled.
In a certain sense we are called upon to take, in leg-

islation, what our Democratic friends style a 'new departure.' The questions of slavery, of the integrity of the Union, of reconstruction, and the like, are hereafter to live mostly, if not wholly, in the memory, soon, we trust, to be erased even from its tablet, in the closer, more cordial fraternity, the better civilization, the general prosperity and high advancement in everything which exalts and refines a nation, for all which, with wise and just government to foster and aid, the costly experience of the last few years has laid the sure foundation.

"With the adjustment of old difficulties comes the era of peace, leaving the people free for the pursuit of avocations which respect their material interests. He is a poor statesman who imagines for a moment that the record of the past, however brilliant or beneficent, can cover present dereliction of duty, or atone for want of fidelity, capacity, and adaptation to grapple successfully with the questions which now confront us. No party can or ought to command the confidence and support of the people which is not equal and faithful to current duties and responsibilities, and whose representatives do not demonstrate by wise action that they exercise their trust broadly, intelligently, effectively, and honestly in the interest of the whole people. He scans the political horizon to little purpose who does not discern this sure sign of the times."

THE SALARY GRAB.

A few days after the passage of the act known as the "Salary Grab Law," Mr. Wheeler wrote to the Secretary of the Treasury : "As this measure was opposed by my vote in all its stages, it does not comport with my views of consistency or propriety to take the above sum to my personal use. I desire, therefore, without giving publicity to the act, to return it to the treasury, which I do by enclosing herewith five-twenty bonds of the United States, purchased with said funds and assigned by me to you for the sole purpose of cancellation." Mr. Wheeler is said to have been the first to adopt this mode of returning his extra pay into the treasury.

WAR RECORD.

When the old Whig party wavered, and finally broke in the onset with slavery, Mr. Wheeler was among the first to hail the new party of freedom. He threw himself with characteristic vigor into the campaign of 1856, with the loss of which by the friends of freedom went out the last hope of averting civil war. His sympathy with the victims of border ruffianism in Kansas, was due in part to the conviction that they were in reality the picket line in the great conflict shortly coming on between slavery and freedom. But his sympathy and his conviction are revealed in this letter : —

TREMONT HOUSE, CHICAGO, *June* 2, 1856.

Editors of the Chicago Daily Tribune : —

Herewith I send draft on Metropolitan Bank, New York, for one hundred dollars, which I will thank you to hand to the appropriate committee for distributing material aid to our hunted and oppressed brethren in Kansas. Residing in the State of New York, to which I shall not return for several days, I am induced to contribute my mite here, that it may be made available as soon as possible. I shall always number among the cherished events of my life, that I had the opportunity of attending the meeting in this city on Saturday evening last. To see here, in the residence of Douglass, such a breaking away from party trammels; such a spontaneous and hearty outburst of sympathetic freedom, and of determined resistance to oppression and wrong, makes one more hopeful for the future, and is an encouraging indication that the free North is at last aroused, and will assert and maintain its just rights in the government. . . . . Now that the banner is thrown to the breeze, there will be no faltering in its support. Kansas will inevitably become free. Slavery has made its last stride. . . . .

W. A. WHEELER.

A few days after the firing on Sumter, a meeting of the citizens of Malone was held, at which Mr. Wheeler made a stirring appeal to his fellow-citizens to sustain the government, and headed a subscription for the relief of soldiers' families with $1000. During the two following years he was in Congress, where he was among the foremost in devising and urging ways and means for the successful prosecution of the war. He also gave a large amount of time and attention to caring for the soldiers from his State, making use of his extensive banking connections to forward their earnings to their families, and in every possible way, contributing to their comfort and looking after their interests. If soldiers' gratitude could be quarried, Mr. Wheeler's bundles of letters contain enough to make a pyramid.

THE LOUISIANA ADJUSTMENT.

Probably the one act of Mr. Wheeler's life which comes nearest to furnishing a measure of the real power and greatness of the man, is his management of the Louisiana difficulties in 1875. This is often referred to as the "Wheeler compromise." But it was not in the ordinary sense of the term a compromise; Mr. Wheeler himself does not so style it; but an adjustment, a plan which aimed first to determine what was just between the two contending parties and then to bring both parties to accept it. The situation was one of the angriest and most threatening among all the scenes which have attended the progress of reconstruction at the South. Intimidation and proscription of the colored voting population on the one side, false returns and military interference on the other; two hostile factions with inflammable Southern passions already heated to madness; leaders on both sides eager to head, but unable to guide their followers; the semblance of a legislature in session and therefore no colorable pretext existing for calling in Federal aid to meet the progress of sedition; here were all the elements of a revolution in which violence and atrocity would have run full riot. Where was the hand that could stay the disaster, and bring these wild elements into harmony? Was there a man in the nation who, answering Virgil's description, revered for his piety and services, could "soothe with sober words their angry mood," and lay this storm of sectional and political passion? It would be hazardous to say that there was more than one : one, happily, there was. Mr. Wheeler, having by means of his position on the Committee on Southern Affairs become thoroughly informed of the facts in the case, first decided in his own mind upon a plan of adjustment, and then went to New Orleans and laid it before the most ultra men of both parties, urging it upon them with all the force of cogent reasoning and strong appeal. Having secured the assent of the leaders, his next and harder task was to bring over the masses of the two parties to accept the plan proposed. While this was in process, Mr. Wheeler remained in New Orleans during a long month of toil and peril, exposed to popular insult, threatened with assassination, on one occasion actually fired on, but holding firmly to his original scheme against all appeals for modifications urged upon him, now by one side, now by the other, until the adjustment was finally effected, and Louisiana had peace. And be it understood that in all this Mr. Wheeler, though a member of the Committee of Congress on Southern Affairs, was clothed with no authority to enforce his views. The settlement he effected cannot even be called an arbitration, for the contending parties had not agreed to submit their differences to him. It was the case of a citizen of the United States going to the rescue of his fellow citizens involved in difficulty and persuading them to accept deliverance at his hands. And never before in our history has one man so changed the condition and prospects of a whole State as did Mr. Wheeler in Louisiana, though acting unofficially, and carrying his measures by sheer force of character. It is pleasant to be able to add that during a subsequent visit to New Orleans, made for the purpose of aiding the execution of his plan, Mr. Wheeler found himself the applauded and fêted hero of that brilliant city, the two parties vying with each in doing him homage.

AS RAILROAD MANAGER.

In endeavoring to give some continuity to the account of Mr. Wheeler's political career, we have passed by a large section of his life during which he devoted himself to business pursuits. He was cashier of the Malone Bank from 1851 to 1865. In 1854, he was appointed one of the trustees of the second mortgage bonds of the old Northern Railroad, which has since been merged in the Ogdensburg and Lake Champlain Railroad. As president of the Board of Trustees, he was virtually manager of the road for eleven years. When it first came into his hands, the bonds were selling for four and five cents on the dollar; but obtaining a decree of the court allowing the trustees to bid in the road, he raised the property for the benefit of the bondholders, until every dollar of the bonds was paying a fair interest to the holders. Mr. Wheeler himself never owned a dollar of the securities of the road. On laying down his trust in 1865, his accounts for the total period of his trusteeship were audited and allowed by the Supreme Court, and he was fully discharged by decree of the court, to which all persons interested were made parties.

RELIGIOUS CHARACTER.

For many years past, Mr. Wheeler has been a member of the Congregational church in Malone. He maintains worship in his family, takes part in the devotional meetings of his church, and is earnest in all Christian activities and benevolences. As, however, he is broader than his party in politics, so his religious sympathies extend beyond his own denomination in the Church. A few years ago, when the Methodists of Malone built a new church edifice, Mr. Wheeler gave $1000 to aid the enterprise. Other denominations have also had from him liberal testimonials of his interest in their prosperity.

PERSONAL TRAITS.

Mr. Wheeler has a dignified and commanding presence; his manners are cordial; his conversation is unusually interesting, as that of a man who has seen and thought much, and who takes pleasure in sharing his views with others. His face has an expression of mingled sternness and sweetness, saying to you at the first look, " Here is a man whom no one would dare ask to do wrong," and at the second look, " Here is a man of whom any one may ask a kindness."

A REPRESENTATIVE MAN.

Take him for all in all, Mr. Wheeler is a representative American. His political principles are grounded in the fundamental ideas of American Republicanism. He is in cordial sympathy with the people and is an exponent of their best spirit and purpose. Endowed with faculties whose combination begets that rarest intelligence which in private life we call good sense and in a statesman wisdom ; raised by education to the level of our ablest men in self-respect and in the power to maintain opinions in their presence, and yet not lifted out of the associations and sympathies of the common people ; a man of such rare purity of character that although he has been in public office nearly all his life, his reputation, even in these scandalous times, is unsullied by even the breath of suspicion ; a " plain man," a true gentleman, a wise statesman, a sincere Christian, Mr. Wheeler is a man singularly fitted, in this time of revived national spirit, to represent the American people and the results of a century of American institutions, in one of the two national offices directly in the gift of the people. May they not lose their opportunity !

LETTER OF ACCEPTANCE.

MALONE, *July* 15, 1876.

Hon. Edward McPherson, and others of the Committee of the Republican National Convention :—

GENTLEMEN :—I received, on the 6th inst., your communication advising me that I had been unanimously nominated by the National Convention of the Republican party, held at Cincinnati on the 14th ult., for the office of Vice-President of the United States; and requesting my acceptance of the same, and asking my attention to the summary of Republican doctrines contained in the platform adopted by the convention.

A nomination made with such unanimity implies a confidence on the part of the Convention which inspires my profound gratitude. It is accepted with a sense of the responsibility which may follow. If elected, I shall endeavor to perform the duties of the office in the fear of the Supreme Ruler, and in the interest of the whole country.

To the summary of doctrines enunciated by the Convention I give my cordial assent. The Republican party has intrenched in the organic law of our land the doctrine that liberty is the supreme, unchangeable law for every foot of American soil. It is the mission of that party to give full effect to this principle by "securing to every American citizen complete liberty and exact equality in the exercise of all civil, political, and public rights." This will be accomplished only when the American citizen, without regard to color, shall wear this panoply of citizenship as fully and as securely in the cane brakes of Louisiana as on the banks of the St. Lawrence.

Upon the question of our Southern relations, my views were recently expressed as a member of the Committee of the United States House of Representatives upon Southern Affairs. Those views remain unchanged, and were thus expressed : —

"We of the North delude ourselves in expecting that the masses of the South, so far behind in many of the attributes of enlightened improvement and civilization, are, in the brief period of ten or fifteen years, to be transformed into our model Northern communities. That can only come through a long course of patient waiting, to which no one can now set certain bounds. There will be a good deal of unavoidable friction, which will call for forbearance, and which will have to be relieved by the temperate, fostering care of the government. One of the most potent, if not indispensable agencies in this direction, will be the devising of some system to aid in the education of the masses. The fact that there are whole counties in Louisiana in which there is not a solitary school-house, is full of suggestion. We compelled these people to remain in the Union, and now duty and interest demand that we leave no just means untried to make them good, loyal citizens. How to diminish the friction, how to stimulate the elevation of this portion of our country, are problems addressing themselves to our best and wisest statesmanship. The foundation for these efforts must be laid in satisfying the Southern people that they are to have equal, exact justice accorded to them. Give them, to the fullest extent, every blessing which the government confers upon the most favored — give them no just cause for complaint, and then hold them, by every necessary means, to an exact, rigid observance of all their duties and obligations under the Constitution and its amendments to secure to *all* within their borders manhood and citizenship, with every right thereto belonging."

The just obligations to public creditors, created when the government was in the throes of threatened dissolution, and as an indispensable condition of its salvation — guarantied by the lives and blood of thousands of its brave defenders — are to be kept with religious faith, as are all the pledges subsidiary thereto and confirmatory thereof.

In my judgment the pledge of Congress of January 14, 1875, for the redemption of the notes of the United States in coin, is the plighted faith of the nation, and national honor, simple honesty, and justice to the people whose permanent welfare and prosperity are dependent upon true money, as the basis of their pecuniary transactions, all demand the scrupulous observance of this pledge, and it is the duty of Congress to supplement it with such legislation as shall be necessary for its strict fulfillment.

In our system of government intelligence must give safety and value to the ballot. Hence the common schools of the land should be preserved in all their vigor, while in accordance with the spirit of the constitution, they and all their endowments should be secured by every possible and proper guaranty against every form of sectarian influence or control.

There should be the strictest economy in the expenditures of the government consistent with its effective administration, and all unnecessary offices should be abolished. Offices should be conferred only upon the basis of high character and particular fitness, and should be admistered only as public trusts, and not for private advantage.

The foregoing are chief among the cardinal principles of the Republican party, and to carry them into full, practical effect is the work it now has in hand. To the completion of its great mission we address ourselves in hope and confidence, cheered and stimulated by the recollection of its past achievements; remembering that, under God, it is to that party that we are indebted in this centennial year of our existence for a preserved, unbroken Union ; for the fact that there is no master or slave throughout our broad domains, and that emancipated millions look upon the ensign of the Republic as the symbol of the fulfilled declaration that all men are created free and equal, and the guaranty of their own equality, under the law, with the most highly favored citizen of the land.

To the intelligence and conscience of all who desire good government, good will, good money, and universal prosperity, the Republican party, not unmindful of the imperfection and short-comings of human organizations, yet with the honest purpose of its masses promptly to retrieve all errors and to summarily punish all offenders against the laws of the country, confidently submits its claims for the continued support of the American people.

Respectfully,

WILLIAM A. WHEELER.

Political and Philosophical Works.

THE NATION:

The Foundations of Civil Order and Political Life in the United States. By E. Mulford. In one volume, 8vo, *cloth*, $2.50.

This work, which was published in the spring of 1870, has steadily gained ground in the opinion of scholars and thoughtful men, and is forcing itself, by the weight of its contents, upon the notice of all students in politics and history.

It is obvious that the book contains more thought, and will give rise to more, than any American book that has been written. — *Eli K. Price, Philadelphia, Pennsylvania.*

No book in its theme remotely approaching Mr. Mulford's in profundity with exhaustiveness has ever before appeared in the English language. — *W. T. Harris, in the St. Louis Journal of Education.*

It is the most valuable contribution to political philosophy which has been written in the English language in this generation. — *James B. Angell, President of the University of Michigan.*

CONSTITUTIONAL LAW.

An Introduction to the Constitutional Law of the United States. Especially designed for the use of Students, General and Professional. By John Norton Pomeroy, LL. D., Dean of the Law School, and Griswold Professor of Political Science in the University of New York, author of an "Introduction to Municipal Law." Third edition, revised, enlarged, and improved. 8vo, *law sheep*, $5.00.

The work in my judgment is a very valuable contribution to the study of Constitutional Law, and to the right understanding of the national Constitution. That great instrument, interpreted from time to time in reference to particular cases, by a tribunal not always composed of the same men, but always of men of various sympathies, associations, and bias, has not always received consistent construction; and a general and comprehensive review of this construction, in connection with the criticism of an independent and enlightened mind, cannot fail to be useful. Your book does this; but I trust it is not to be the end of your labors in this direction. — *Chief Justice S. P. Chase of the U. S. Supreme Court.*

POLITICAL PARTIES.

An Inquiry into the Origin and Course of Political Parties in the United States. By the late ex-President Martin Van Buren. 8vo, *cloth*, $3.00.

. . . In a word, this work is the only reliable history of political parties that we have. We, of course, except and excuse its Democratic partialities, for its author was bound to be true to his instincts. Aside from an appearance of prolixity, which is however but a minuteness of detail, the rise and progress of the great political parties that have held the reins of the government are clearly delineated. — *Baltimore Journal of Commerce.*

PUBLISHED BY

HURD AND HOUGHTON, 13 ASTOR PLACE, NEW YORK;

The Riverside Press, Cambridge.

WORKS OF W. D. HOWELLS.

Standard Books for the Library

PUBLISHED BY

HURD AND HOUGHTON, New York.

𝕿𝖍𝖊 𝕽𝖎𝖛𝖊𝖗𝖘𝖎𝖉𝖊 𝕻𝖗𝖊𝖘𝖘, 𝕮𝖆𝖒𝖇𝖗𝖎𝖉𝖌𝖊.

———

ANDERSEN'S (Hans Christian) COMPLETE WORKS. 10 vols.,
  cr. 8vo $16.50
BACON'S WORKS. 15 vols., cr. 8vo........................... 33.75
CARLYLE'S CRITICAL AND MISCELLANEOUS ESSAYS. 4
  vols., cr. 8vo.. 9.00
CHINESE CLASSICS. WORKS OF CONFUCIUS AND MEN-
  CIUS. 1 vol., 8vo.. 3.50
COOPER'S (J. Fenimore) COMPLETE WORKS.
  Riverside Edition. 32 vols., cr. 8vo................... 72.00
  Household Edition. 32 vols., 16mo..................... 40.00
COOPER'S SEA TALES. 10 vols., 16mo...................... 12.50
COOPER'S LEATHER STOCKING TALES. 5 vols.
  Riverside Edition. Cr. 8vo........................... 11.25
  Household Edition. 16mo.............................. 6.25
DE QUINCEY'S COMPLETE WORKS. 12 vols., cr. 8vo 21.00
DICKENS' (Charles) COMPLETE WORKS. *Five Editions.*
  New Household Edition. 56 vols., 559 illustrations. 16mo.......... 84.00
  Illustrated Library Edition. 29 vols., 559 illustrations. Cr. 8vo.... 58.00
  Riverside Edition. 28 vols., 559 illustrations. Cr. 8vo............. 49.00
  Globe Edition. 15 vols., 55 illustrations. 12mo................... 18.50
  Large Paper Edition. 55 vols., 559 illustrations. Large 8vo.......275.00
GREENE. LIFE OF NATHANIEL GREENE, MAJOR-GEN-
  ERAL IN THE ARMY OF THE REVOLUTION. 3 vols., 8vo 12.00
KNIGHT'S AMERICAN MECHANICAL DICTIONARY 3 vols.,
  8vo.. 24.00
MACAULAY'S HISTORY OF ENGLAND.
  Riverside Edition. 8 vols., cr. 8vo................... 16.00
  Student's Edition.................................... 8.00
MACAULAY'S CRITICAL, HISTORICAL, AND MISCELLA-
  NEOUS ESSAYS, WITH A MEMOIR.
  Riverside Edition. 6 vols., cr. 8vo.................. 12.00
  Student's Edition. 3 vols., cr. 8vo................. 6.00
  Popular Edition. 1 vol., cr. 8vo.................... 2.50
MACAULAY'S SPEECHES AND POEMS, WITH PAPERS UPON
  THE INDIAN PENAL CODE.
  Riverside Edition. 2 vols., cr. 8vo................. 4.00
  Student's Edition. 1 vol., cr. 8vo................. 2.00
MONTAIGNE'S WORKS. 4 vols., cr. 8vo.................... 9.00
SCOTT'S WAVERLEY NOVELS. 25 vols., cr. 8vo............ 37.50
SMITH'S (Dr. William) DICTIONARY OF THE BIBLE. *Amer-
  ican Edition*, UNABRIDGED, ENLARGED, AND COR-
  RECTED. 4 vols., 8vo.................................. 26.00
"In short, it seems that we have to thank America for the most com-
plete work of the kind in the English, or, indeed, in any other language."
— *London Bookseller.*

** The above prices are for cloth bindings, but all of these books
are sold also in fine library bindings.

A complete Catalogue of the Riverside Press publications will be
sent to any address on application to

HURD AND HOUGHTON, 13 Astor Place, New York.

𝕿𝖍𝖊 𝕽𝖎𝖛𝖊𝖗𝖘𝖎𝖉𝖊 𝕻𝖗𝖊𝖘𝖘, 𝕮𝖆𝖒𝖇𝖗𝖎𝖉𝖌𝖊.